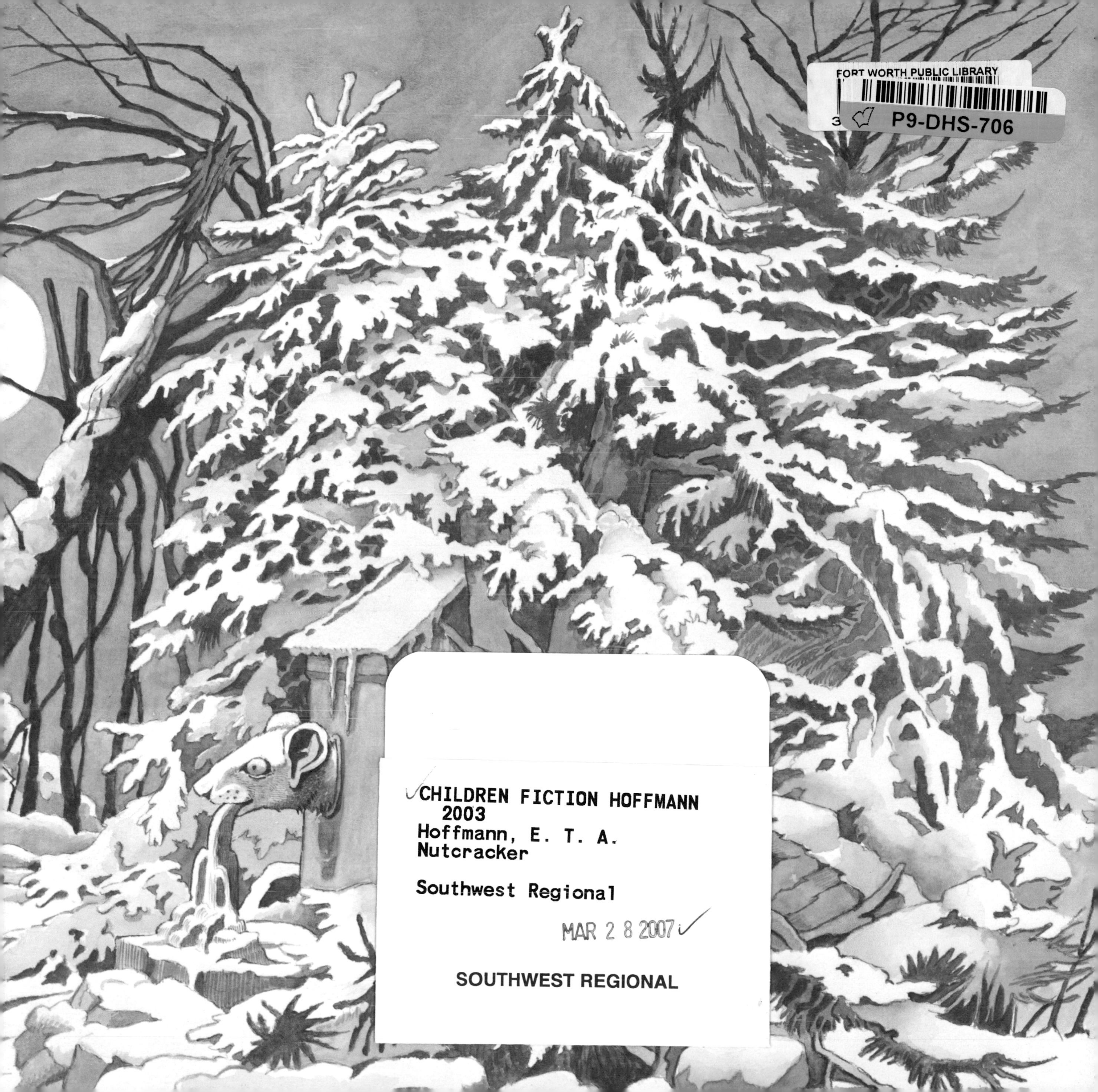

NUTCRACKER

E.T.A. HOFFMANN

NUTCRACKER

TRANSLATED BY

PICTURES BY

MAURICE SENDAK

GRAMERCY BOOKS

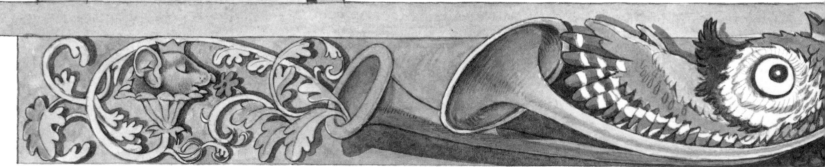

FFMANN

ACKER

RALPH MANHEIM

ES BY

SENDAK

KS · NEW YORK

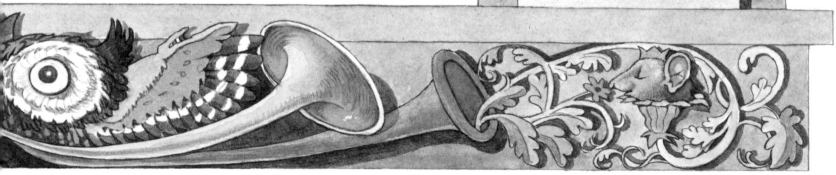

Book design by Ken Sansone

This 2003 edition published by Gramercy Books, an imprint of
Random House Value Publishing, a division of Random House, Inc., New York.

Gramercy is a registered trademark and the colophon
is a trademark of Random House, Inc.

Printed in Japan

Random House
New York • Toronto • London • Sydney • Auckland
www.randomhouse.com

Library of Congress Cataloging in Publication data

Hoffmann, E. T. A. (Ernst-Theodor Amadeus), 1776–1822.
Nutcracker

Translation of: Nussknacker Und Mausekönig.

[1. Fairy Tales] I. Sendak, Maurice, ILL.
II. Manheim, Ralph, 1907-1992   III. Title.
PZ8. H675NV   1984   [Fic]   83-25266
ISBN 0-517-55285-X

10   9   8   7   6

To
Francia Russell, who thought of it
Kent Stowell, who shaped it
and
the dancers of the Pacific Northwest Ballet,
who made it happen

Contents

Introduction

M Y IMMEDIATE REACTION to the request that I design *Nutcracker* was negative. The offer came early in 1981 from Kent Stowell, artistic director of the Pacific Northwest Ballet. I was flattered, but my reasons for saying no were plentiful and precise. To begin with, who in the world needed another *Nutcracker*? The mandatory Christmas tree and Candyland sequences were enough to sink my spirits completely. And the fantastical subject mixed generously with children seemed, paradoxically, too suited to me, too predictable. I didn't *want* to be suited to the confectionery goings-on of this, I thought, most bland and banal of ballet productions. Finally, and most seriously, after only three operas and one off-Broadway musical for children, I didn't have a clue about how to approach a ballet. Where would I find the time to design a giant production—two full acts and over 180 costumes?

Of course I did it. We did it together. Most of my doubts and worries were put to rest when Kent and I met for the first time early in 1981 in New York City. I liked him immediately for *not* wanting me to do *Nutcracker* for all the obvious reasons but rather because he wished me to join him in a leap into the unknown. He suggested we abandon the

predictable *Nutcracker* and find a fresh version that did honor to Hoffmann, Tchaikovsky, and ourselves.

Later that year Kent invited me to Seattle to see the company's old *Nutcracker*. By then I had fallen in love with the project and after that Christmas of 1981, I set to work in earnest.

There is no question of the ballet's appeal; as far as most audiences are concerned it works even in an indifferent production. But, like many before us, we felt that the ballet needed renovation. What is potentially dramatic in Act One is dissipated in the carnival atmosphere of Act Two. How to dramatically bridge the two acts and focus fierce attention on our heroine Clara (Marie, in the book) became the exciting goal.

My first step was to return to the source: E.T.A. Hoffmann who, in 1816, wrote the amazing long short story called *The Nutcracker and the Mouse King*. I was astonished at my difficulty in locating an English version of this most well known of his tales. When I finally did find it in *The Best Tales of E.T.A. Hoffmann* (Dover, 1967), I read the story greedily. The result of that reading was confusion. There was a vast difference between the original tale and what took place on the stage.

Jack Anderson's book *The Nutcracker Ballet* helped unravel some of the mystery. The scenario of the ballet is a hybrid concocted in 1891 by Ivan Alexandrovitch Vsevolojsky, director of the Imperial Theater in St.

Petersburg, and Marius Petipa, the choreographer, both of whom had been Tchaikovsky's collaborators on *The Sleeping Beauty*.

Rather than turning directly to Hoffmann, these artists based their scenario on a popular French version of the tale by Alexandre Dumas, *père, The Nutcracker of Nuremberg*. When Vsevolojsky simplified the Dumas even further for the stage, it emerged at a dangerous distance from Hoffmann. Why, one wonders, did these men ever choose such an unlikely candidate in the first place? The original is too long and full of complicated digressions to have made a coherent ballet. But their version, familiar to audiences today, is smoothed out, bland, and utterly devoid not only of difficulties but of the weird, dark qualities that make it something of a masterpiece.

Tchaikovsky, understandably disappointed in the scenario, proceeded to compose a score that in overtone and erotic suggestion is happily closer to Hoffmann than Dumas. His music, bristling with implied action, has a subtext alive with wild child cries and belly noises. It is rare and genuine and does justice to the private world of children. One can, after all, count on the instincts of a genius.

The problem dramatically, as Kent and I saw it, was that the vital subplot, the tale within a tale in Hoffmann's story, was entirely missing from the ballet. "The Story of the Hard Nut" gives the fairy tale dramatic sense and needed psychological meaning. Its absence in the ballet leaves the center critically vacant. We were not so foolish or vain as to imagine that we could totally solve this problem, but we were determined to incorporate as much as we could of the entire original story into our scenario. This was not a matter of pedantry or even of faithfulness to Hoffmann. It was to enable us to bring the middle of the ballet to life.

There are odd, magical means by which one eases oneself or talks oneself into a project. When I began *Nutcracker* I was beady-eyed, looking for a proper sign. It came from Herr E.T.A. Hoffmann himself, who out of love for that most lovable and best of all artists, Mozart, changed one of his middle names to Amadeus. Tchaikovsky adored Mozart and had written a number of compositions in homage to this master and my own particular hero. So there he was, smack in the middle of this production, the great papa, so to speak, of all involved.

Although my early storyboards and rough cardboard models gave me no hint as to where and when I would set my *Nutcracker*, I began to realize that it had long been set in my unconscious. The magic triumvirate of Mozart, Hoffmann, and Schinkel, the great nineteenth-century German architect, had already led me to place the ballet in the period they shared, 1790–1830. The rich, exotic, yet strict lines of neoclassic design and costume perfectly suited my vision of Clara and her world.

Kent and I were drawn to Clara in different ways. I endowed her with the wisdom and strength I conjure up to endow all my children and then surrounded her with a minefield of problems. Kent saw her as a child older than Hoffmann's seven-year-old Marie. Together we created a prepubescent twelve-year-old, all nerves and curiosity devouring the world with her eyes and imagination, just awaking to her first wonderful, fearful, erotic sensations. The stage became her half-real, half-nightmare battleground. The drama grew naturally as we watched Clara, frightened yet exuberant, cross that battleground.

Because there was neither time, music, nor space to tell the whole complicated story we reduced it to a brief, symbolic, and, we hope, effective episode. It was essential that the peculiar relationship between Clara and Drosselmeier be clearly drawn. The little scene we invented chillingly encapsulated Clara's nightmare vision of that half-child, half-man. It introduced Princess Pirlipat of the tale within a tale and made crucial connections between her and Clara and the Nutcracker prince. To accomplish all this in roughly three minutes we desperately needed more music.

On one of my working trips to Seattle I enthusiastically introduced Kent to Tchaikovsky's opera *The Queen of Spades* and pointed out a moment in the opera, a charmingly concocted pastiche of Mozart, that I felt might work beautifully. As always, without a single false flourish, Kent seized this critical moment and brought it to theatrical life. And so Mozart appeared twice in our *Nutcracker*, graphically as a bust on top of Clara's toy cabinet and musically as a divertissement in the middle of the Stahlbaum's Christmas party.

For our finale, Kent and I firmly decided against the most obligatory of all obligatory scenes, The Land of Sweets. In Hoffmann it is only a short, ironical interlude. The spirit of our scenario led elsewhere. But where? After some missteps I consulted with Frank Corsaro, the ingenious stage director, my collaborator and teacher. He forced me simply to face the inner logic of our script and to march bravely where it led us—to an eighteenth-century seraglio, full of exaggerated glee and erotic conceits typical of that period. Of course, there is no seraglio in Hoffmann's tale, but once again Kent and I chose to follow the quintessential, rather than the literal, Hoffmann.

Fidelity to Hoffmann's spirit has also been my guide in this illustrated version of *Nutcracker*. In changing hats from designer to illustrator I have been faced with a curious dilemma. After all, there are whole sequences in the tale itself that never appear on the stage. Rather than adjust these designs to fit the book, I decided to completely illustrate "The Story of the Hard Nut." Because of this decision the pictures for this book are composed of two separate entities. There are the designs and costumes from the ballet version and then the fresh pictures done specifically for the tale. In addition, there are a few to animate the original stage designs and a few more that I could not or would not resist doing. This may explain some disparity in style and tone from section to section. I hope that despite this I have done some justice to Hoffmann and, above all, have not betrayed the mad spirit of his mad story.

One last word concerning the translation. To quote E. F. Bleiler, editor of the Dover edition, "(Hoffmann) translators all too often have rendered him into an English that is complex, curious and sometimes tedious. This . . . resulted in the loss of three of his greatest gifts . . . nervous energy, hard clarity of expression and narrative flow. . . . This present volume . . . is best considered an interim edition, prepared to satisfy a need until something better emerges." When Crown Publishers invited Ralph Manheim to translate this work, something far better emerged. E.T.A. Hoffmann's *The Nutcracker and the Mouse King* has finally been brought fully and faithfully to life in English. I feel fortunate to be allied with this literary event.

The premiere of *Nutcracker* in December 1983, in Seattle, was a superb moment for Kent, the company, and me. While we see the flaws and wince at the near misses, we are satisfied that our individual creative selves have found a comfortable and handsome partnership in this vast, unwieldy work. It is, from the opening bars of Marie's dream, to the unpredictable apotheosis, truly our *Nutcracker*.

MAURICE SENDAK
April 1984
Ridgefield, Connecticut

NUTCRACKER

Christmas Eve

O N THE TWENTY-FOURTH of December Dr. Stahlbaum's children were not allowed to set foot in the small family parlor, much less the adjoining company parlor—not at any time during the day. Fritz and Marie sat huddled together in a corner of the little back room. An eerie feeling came over them when dusk fell and, as usual on Christmas Eve, no light was brought in. In whispers Fritz told his younger sister (she had just turned seven) that since early morning he had heard murmuring and shuffling and muffled hammer blows in the locked rooms. And a short while before, he confided, a small, dark man had crept down the hallway with a big box under his arm, and he, Fritz, felt pretty sure that this could only be Godfather Drosselmeier. At that, Marie clapped her little hands for joy and cried out:

"Oh, what do you think Godfather Drosselmeier has made for us?"

Judge Drosselmeier was anything but handsome. He was short and very thin, his face was seamed with wrinkles, he had a big black patch where his right eye should have been, and he had no hair at all, for which reason he wore a beautiful white wig, a real work of art. And Judge Drosselmeier was himself a skilled craftsman, able to make and repair

1

clocks. When one of the fine clocks in the Stahlbaum house was sick and unable to sing, Godfather Drosselmeier would come over, remove his glass wig and yellow coat, and put on a blue apron. For a while he would stick sharp instruments into the clock. Little Marie felt real pain at the sight. But it didn't hurt the clock in the least; on the contrary, it came back to life and made everyone happy by whirring and striking and singing merrily. Whenever he came, he had something in his pocket for the children—now a little man who would roll his eyes and bow in a most comical way, now a box that a little bird would hop out of, now something else. But every year at Christmas he took great pains to turn out a work of wonderful artistry, so precious that the children's parents always put it away in a safe place.

"Oh," Marie cried out, "what do you think Godfather Drosselmeier has made for us?"

Fritz said it was sure to be a fortress, with all kinds of soldiers marching up and down and drilling, and then other soldiers would come and try to get in, but the brave defenders would fire their guns, which would boom and thunder wonderfully.

"No, no," Marie interrupted. "Godfather Drosselmeier said something to me about a beautiful garden with a big lake in it and lovely swans with golden necklaces swimming around on it and singing the most beautiful songs. And then a little girl comes across the garden to the lake and calls the swans and feeds them marzipan."

"Swans don't eat marzipan," said Fritz rather rudely, "and besides, Godfather Drosselmeier can't make a whole garden. And anyway, what good are his toys to us? They always get taken away before we know it. I like the things Mama and Papa give us a lot better, because we can keep them and do what we like with them."

Then the children tried to guess what their parents would give them this time. Marie remarked that Mistress Trude (her big doll) had changed for the worse. Clumsier than ever, she kept falling on the floor, which always left nasty marks on her face. And no amount of scolding would help, she just couldn't keep her clothes clean. Marie also remembered how Mama had smiled at her for being so delighted with her doll Gretchen's little parasol. Fritz, on the other hand, observed that, as his father was well aware, a decent chestnut horse was needed for his royal stables, and that his army had no cavalry at all.

So the children knew that their parents had bought them all sorts of lovely presents, and were busy imagining them, but they were just as certain that the Christ Child was looking on with tender loving eyes, and that Christmas gifts, because he had blessed them, gave more pleasure than any others. The children, who kept whispering about the presents they expected, were reminded of this by their elder sister, Louise, who added that it was always the Christ Child who, by the hands of their dear parents, brought children things that would give them true enjoyment, since he knew what those would be better than the children themselves. So, big sister Louise went on, instead of hoping and wishing for all sorts of things, they should wait quietly like well-behaved children for whatever the Christ Child would bring.

Marie sat deep in thought, but Fritz muttered, "All the same, I'd like a chestnut horse and some hussars."

By then it was very dark. Fritz and Marie pressed close together, afraid to say another word; they had a feeling that gentle wings were passing over, and they seemed to hear beautiful music in the distance. When a flash of brightness flitted across the wall, they knew it was the Christ Child flying away on glowing clouds to other happy children.

At that moment a silvery-bright bell rang ding-a-ling, the doors flew open, and such a flood of light streamed in from the big parlor that the children cried aloud, "Oh! Oh!" and stood stock-still on the threshold. Papa and Mama appeared in the doorway, took their children by the hand, and said, "Come in, come in, dear children, and see what the Christ Child has brought you."

The Presents

KIND READER OR LISTENER—Fritz, Theodore, Ernst, or whatever your name may be—I must ask you to think as hard as you can of your last Christmas table piled high with gifts. Then perhaps you will be able to conjure up the scene: how the children stood silent with shining eyes, and how after quite some time Marie heaved a sigh and cried out, "Oh, how lovely! Oh, how lovely!" and Fritz took two or three rather spectacular jumps into the air.

The children must have been especially well behaved that year, for they had never before received so many splendid presents. The big Christmas tree in the middle of the room was decorated with any number of gold and silver apples, and sugared almonds, bright-colored candles, and goodies of all kinds shaped like buds and blossoms hung from every branch. But the most startling thing about this wonderful tree was that hundreds of tapers glittered like stars in its dark branches, and the tree itself, shining with an inner light, invited the children to pick its blossoms and fruits. Round about the tree everything glittered splendidly—no one could even have described all those wonderful things. Marie discovered the prettiest dolls and all sorts of shiny little utensils.

Best of all, a little silk dress, decorated with colored ribbons, had been hung up in such a way that she could examine it from all sides. And examine it she did, crying out time after time, "Oh, what a beautiful, oh what a lovely dress; and I know, I know for sure that I'll be allowed to put it on."

Meanwhile, Fritz galloped around the table three or four times, trying out the new horse that, true enough, he had found already bridled on the table. On dismounting, he remarked that the beast was rather wild, but it didn't matter, he'd break him in. Then he reviewed his new squadron of hussars, who were admirably fitted out in red and gold uniforms, with silver sabers and mounts so gleaming white that they too seemed to be of pure silver. When the children had calmed down a little, they got ready to look at the picture books that lay open, showing all sorts of beautiful flowers and people clothed in many colors and dear little children at play, all painted to look as natural as if they were really alive and talking.

Well, the children were just getting ready to look at these wonderful books when the bell rang again. Knowing that Godfather Drosselmeier would be unveiling his present, they ran to the table that had been set up beside the wall. The screen that had hidden it was taken away, and what did the children see? On a green lawn, bright with flowers, stood a magnificent castle with dozens of sparkling windows and golden towers. Chimes were playing, doors and windows opened, and tiny but shapely ladies and gentlemen wearing long dresses and plumed hats could be seen strolling around the rooms. In the central hall the silver chandeliers had so many candles in them that they seemed to be all afire, and children in little skirts and doublets were dancing to the music of the chimes. A man in an emerald-green cloak kept appearing at one of the windows, waving his hand and vanishing, and Godfather Drosselmeier himself, who was hardly bigger than Papa's thumb, would come out from time to time and stand at the castle gate for a while and go back in again.

Bracing his arms on the table, Fritz looked for a while at the beautiful castle and at the dancing and walking figures. Then he said, "Godfather Drosselmeier, let me go inside your castle."

"Impossible," said the Judge. And he was right, for it was foolish of Fritz to think of going into a castle that, golden towers and all, was not as high as himself. This Fritz understood, but after a while, when the ladies and gentlemen continued to stroll back and forth, the children to dance, the emerald-green man to appear at the same window, and Godfather Drosselmeier to step outside the door, Fritz said impatiently, "Godfather Drosselmeier, come out of the other door next time."

"That's not possible, dear Fritz," said the Judge.

"Then," said Fritz, "make that green man who keeps coming to the window walk around with the others."

"That too is impossible," said the Judge.

"Then make the children come out," cried Fritz. "I want to look at them close up."

"No no no, all those things are impossible," said the Judge crossly. "That's how the mechanism works, and it can't be changed."

"Is that right?" said Fritz with an affected drawl. "It can't be changed, can it? In that case, Godfather Drosselmeier, if all your precious little people in the castle can do is the same thing over and over again, they don't amount to much, and I don't really care for them. Give me my hussars. They march forward or backward as I command, and they're not shut up in a house."

With that he ran back to the Christmas table and made his squadrons trot this way and that on their silver horses, wheel about, charge, and fire their guns to his heart's content. Marie also quietly crept away, for she too had soon tired of watching the dolls strolling and dancing about inside the castle, although, as she was a good, well-behaved child, she hadn't wanted to show it.

Judge Drosselmeier said rather crossly to the children's parents, "A work of art like this isn't meant for ignorant children. I'm just going to pack my castle up again." But Mrs. Stahlbaum came over and got him to show her the ingenious clockwork that moved the little figures, which meant taking the whole castle apart and putting it back together again. That cheered him up, and he gave the children some lovely brown men and women with gold faces, hands, and legs. They smelled as fragrant as gingerbread, and Fritz and Marie were delighted with them. Sister Louise had been given a lovely dress, which she put on when her mother asked her to, and she looked very pretty in it. But when Marie was asked to put on hers, she said she'd rather just look at it for a while, and she was allowed to do so.

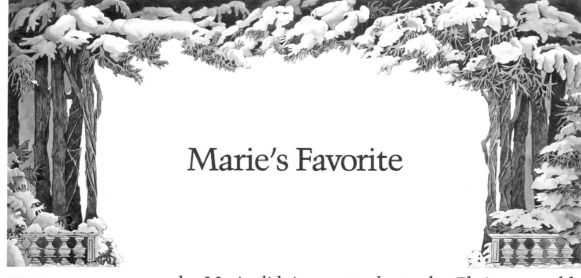

Marie's Favorite

THE REAL REASON why Marie didn't want to leave the Christmas table was that she had just caught sight of something she hadn't noticed before. Fritz's hussars had been parading near the tree. When they marched away, an excellent little man came into view. He stood there quietly, as though patiently waiting his turn.

One might have found fault with his build: his torso was too long and stout for his short, skinny legs, and his head was much too big for the rest of him. But, to make up for these disadvantages, the distinction of his dress showed him to be a man of taste and breeding. He was wearing a well-cut lavender hussar's jacket with lots of white frogging and buttons, breeches of the same stuff, and the daintiest little boots that had ever graced the feet of a student or even an officer. They were molded as neatly to his dainty little legs as if they had been painted on. Oddly enough, though, in view of these fine clothes, he had, hanging from his shoulders, a skimpy, ungainly cloak that looked almost as if it were made of wood, and he was wearing what appeared to be a miner's cap. But Marie remembered that Godfather Drosselmeier often wore a wretched-looking morning coat and a hideous cap, neither of which prevented him from being a dear, sweet godfather. And it also occurred to Marie that even if

Godfather Drosselmeier were to dress as prettily as this little man, he wouldn't be as handsome. With Marie it was love at first sight, and the longer she gazed at the sweet little man, the more delighted she was with his good-natured face. His light green, slightly too prominent eyes were also full of kindness, and his well-curled, white-cotton beard was most becoming, as it brought out the sweet smile of his bright red lips.

"Oh, Father dear," Marie cried out, "who does the dear little man by the tree belong to?"

"Dear child," said Dr. Stahlbaum, "our friend here will serve you all well. He will crack hard nuts for all of you with his teeth, and he belongs to Louise as much as to you and Fritz."

Carefully picking him up from the table, Dr. Stahlbaum lifted his wooden cloak, whereupon the little man opened his mouth wide, revealing two rows of sharp white teeth. At her father's bidding, Marie put in a nut, and—crack—the little man bit it in two, the shell fell down, and Marie found the sweet kernel in her hand.

Dr. Stahlbaum told the children that the pretty little man was descended from the Nutcracker family and practiced the trade of his forebears. Marie cried out for joy, and her father said, "Well, dear Marie, since you seem so fond of friend Nutcracker, he shall be entrusted to your special care, though, as I've already told you, Louise and Fritz have as much right to make use of him as you."

Marie picked him up and gave him nuts to crack, but she chose the smallest so the little man wouldn't have to open his mouth too wide, which did not really become him. Louise joined her, and friend Nutcracker had to work for them both. He seemed glad to do it, for he kept smiling in the friendliest way.

By that time Fritz was tired of riding and maneuvering. Hearing the sound of nuts being cracked, he ran over to his sisters and laughed heartily at the droll little man. After that, Fritz too wanted to eat nuts.

Nutcracker passed from hand to hand and never stopped opening and closing his mouth. Fritz always chose the biggest and hardest nuts, and all of a sudden—crack crack—three little teeth fell out of Nutcracker's mouth, and his lower jaw began to wobble.

"Oh, my poor little Nutcracker!" Marie cried, taking him out of Fritz's hands.

"He's just a stupid fool," said Fritz. "Calls himself a nutcracker and his teeth are no good. He doesn't even know his trade, if you ask me. Give him to me, Marie. Let him crack nuts for me, even if he loses the rest of his teeth and his jaw drops off too. Who cares about a good-for-nothing like him?"

Marie was in tears. "No, no!" she cried. "He's my dear Nutcracker and you can't have him. See the sad way he's looking at me and showing me his sore little mouth. You're a heartless brute—you beat your horses, and you've even had one of your soldiers shot."

"That's the way it has to be," said Fritz. "You don't understand these things. And the Nutcracker belongs to me as much as to you, so hand him over."

Sobbing, Marie wrapped the wounded Nutcracker in her little handkerchief. The children's parents came over with Godfather Drosselmeier, who to Marie's dismay sided with Fritz. But Dr. Stahlbaum said, "I expressly entrusted Nutcracker to Marie's care, which is obviously just what he needs. So there's no point in arguing, she and no one else is in charge of him. What's more, I'm very much surprised at Fritz making demands on a man wounded in the line of duty. As a good soldier, he should know that wounded men are never expected to do active service."

Fritz felt deeply ashamed. Losing all interest in nuts and nutcrackers, he slunk away to the other side of the table, where, after posting the necessary sentries, he sent his hussars into night quarters. Marie collected Nutcracker's lost teeth and bandaged his wounded mouth with a

pretty white ribbon she had taken from her dress. She rocked the poor little fellow, who was looking extremely pale and shaken, in her arms like a baby, meanwhile looking at the pretty pictures in the new picture book that lay there along with the other presents. She grew very angry, which was not at all like her, when Godfather Drosselmeier laughed at her and kept asking why she was making such a fuss over such an ugly fellow. Remembering the strange resemblance between Nutcracker and Drosselmeier, which had struck her at first sight of the little man, she said very gravely, "I'm not at all sure, dear Godfather, that if you were dressed like my dear Nutcracker and were not wearing such shiny boots—I'm not at all sure that you'd look as handsome as he does."

Marie didn't know why her parents laughed so heartily or why the Judge went red in the face and hardly laughed at all. There may have been some special reason.

Strange Happenings

ALONG THE WALL to your left as you enter the Stahlbaums' living room there is a tall glass-fronted cabinet in which the children keep all the lovely presents they receive each year. Louise was still a very small child when her father had this cabinet made by a skillful craftsman, who fitted it out with such sparkling panes of glass and made the whole thing so cleverly that the contents looked almost brighter and more beautiful than when you held them in your hands.

On the top shelf, beyond the reach of Marie and Fritz, were the products of Godfather Drosselmeier's skill; the next shelf down held the picture books. As for the two lowest shelves, Marie and Fritz were allowed to keep whatever they pleased there; Marie used the bottom shelf as a home for her dolls, while Fritz garrisoned his troops on the one above it. That is just what they did today, for while Fritz was installing his hussars on the higher of the two shelves, Marie pushed Mistress Trude to one side, moved her new doll into the beautifully furnished room, and invited herself in to have tea and cakes with her.

I've said that this room was very well furnished, and that's the truth, for, my attentive reader Marie, I don't know whether you, like the little

Stahlbaum girl (you remember, of course, that she too was called Marie)—I don't know, that is, whether you too have a lovely little flowered sofa, several dear little chairs, a charming tea table, and most especially a spanking clean bed for your lovely dolls to sleep in. All those things were in the corner of the shelf, the walls of which were papered with colored pictures. You can imagine that the new doll, whose name, as Marie learned that same evening, was Mistress Clara, found her room extremely comfortable.

IT WAS GETTING LATE—almost midnight. Godfather Drosselmeier had left long ago, and still the children couldn't tear themselves away from the glass-fronted cabinet, though their mother had several times urged them to turn in for the night.

"It's true," Fritz finally said, "the poor fellows"—meaning his hussars—"need their rest." With that he retired. But Marie pleaded, "Just a little while longer, let me stay just a little longer, Mother dear, I still have certain things to attend to, and then I'll go right off to bed."

Marie was a sensible, well-behaved child, so her mother felt that she could leave her alone with her toys for a while without too much cause for worry. Still, to make sure that Marie wouldn't be so intent on her new doll and all the other new toys that she'd forget the candles around the cupboard, her mother put them all out, leaving on only the lamp, which hung from the ceiling in the middle of the room and cast a pleasantly soft light. "Go to bed soon, Marie, or you won't be able to get up tomorrow," said her mother as she went off to her bedroom.

As soon as Marie was alone, she did what had been most on her mind, something that she herself didn't know why, she couldn't mention to her mother. All the while, she had been holding the wounded Nutcracker in her arms, still wrapped in her handkerchief. Now she laid him carefully on the table, unwrapped the handkerchief ever so slowly, and examined his wounds. Nutcracker was very pale, but he gave Marie a sad, friendly smile that went straight to her heart.

"Dear Nutcracker," she said softly, "don't be angry at brother Fritz for hurting you so, he meant no harm. It's just that the rough soldier's life has made him somewhat hardhearted, otherwise he's not a bad boy, I assure you. But now I'm going to take the very best care of you until you're well and happy again. Your teeth will be put back in and held fast, and Godfather Drosselmeier will set your shoulders straight, he's good at those things . . ."

Marie couldn't finish what she had to say, because the moment she mentioned Godfather Drosselmeier, friend Nutcracker made a horrible face and his eyes seemed to send out green sparks. But just as Marie was beginning to be frightened, Nutcracker turned to her with his usual sad smile, and she knew that what had so distorted his face was the light of the lamp, flaring up suddenly in the draft.

"What a foolish girl I am," she said to herself, "getting scared for no reason and even imagining that a wooden doll can make faces. But I do love Nutcracker, because he's so funny and good natured, and I *will* take the best care of him."

With that she picked Nutcracker up in her arms, went over to the toy cabinet, bent down in front of it, and said to her new doll, "Mistress Clara, I must ask you to give up your bed to our poor Nutcracker and make do with the sofa. After all, you're bursting with health, or you wouldn't have such plump red cheeks, and I hope you realize that very few dolls, even the prettiest, have such nice soft sofas to sleep on."

Mistress Clara looked very distinguished and morose in her Christmas finery, and she didn't say boo.

"But why am I making such a fuss?" said Marie. Whereupon she

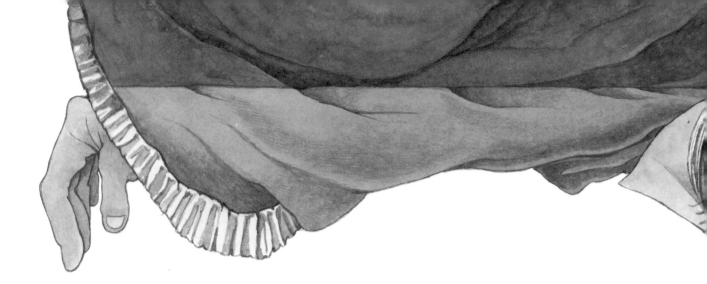

pulled out the bed, put Nutcracker in it gently, took a pretty ribbon that she usually wore around her waist and wrapped it around his injured shoulders, and drew the bedclothes up to his nose.

"I won't have him staying with that horrid Clara," she said to herself, and moved the bed with Nutcracker in it to the shelf above, right next to the pretty little village where Fritz's hussars were quartered for the night. Then she shut the toy cabinet, and she was going to the bedroom when— now pay attention, children!—soft whispering and shuffling were heard round about, behind the stove, behind the chairs, behind the cupboards.

The tall clock whirred louder and louder, but it didn't strike. Marie looked at it and saw that the big gilded owl perched on top of it had lowered its wings in such a way as to cover the whole clock and was sticking out its ugly cat's head with the crooked beak. The whirring grew louder and louder, and now words could be heard:

> *"Clock, clocks, whir softly, do not strike.*
> *Mouse King is keen of hearing. Whir whir purr purr*
> *Sing him the old song whir whir purr purr,*
> *Ring, bell, ring. Ding dong ding dong.*
> *He won't last long."*

And then the clock whirred twelve times—twelve muffled whir whirs.

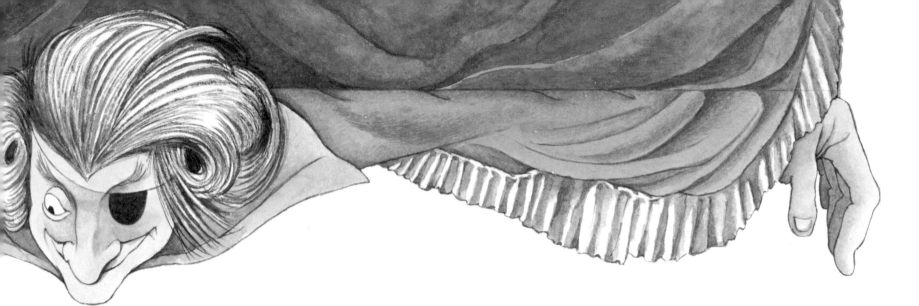

Marie shuddered. She was on the point of running away when she saw Godfather Drosselmeier, who was sitting on the clock instead of the owl. His yellow coattails hung down like drooping wings.

"Godfather Drosselmeier, Godfather Drosselmeier," she cried out. "What are you doing up there? Come down and stop frightening me so, you wicked Godfather Drosselmeier!"

But then she heard giggling and squeaking all around her, followed by the sound of a thousand little feet scampering behind the walls, and a thousand little lights peered out through the cracks in the woodwork. But it wasn't lights, oh no! It was little sparkling eyes, and Marie saw mice peering out on all sides and squeezing through the chinks. Soon they were scampering all over the room, bigger and bigger bands of them, and in the end they formed ranks, just as Fritz's soldiers did before marching off to war.

Marie thought they were funny, and since she did not (like some children) have an inborn horror of mice, she would have lost all fear, had she not suddenly heard a piercing squeak that sent shivers down her spine. And what did she see then? Believe me, dear reader Fritz, I know you're as brave as the wise and fearless field marshal Fritz Stahlbaum, but if you had seen what Marie saw then, you'd have run away. I even think you'd have jumped into bed and pulled the covers higher above your ears.

But poor Marie couldn't do that, because—now listen, dear children—right in front of her feet, sand and lime and crushed stone came gushing out of the floor as though driven by some underground force, and seven mouse heads with seven sparkling crowns rose up, squeaking and squealing hideously. Soon the mouse's body, to which the seven heads were attached, worked itself up through the floor. And this enormous mouse, crowned with seven diadems, was hailed by the entire army, cheering with three loud squeaks. And then the army set itself in motion—hop hop trot trot—heading straight for the toy cabinet, straight for Marie, who was standing right next to it.

Marie's heart beat so hard with fear and horror that she thought it would jump out of her body and she would die. And then she felt as if her blood were standing still in her veins. Close to fainting, she reeled backward, and then—crash!—the glass pane she had struck with her elbow fell in slivers to the floor. For a moment she felt a stinging pain in her left arm, but suddenly her heart was lighter. She no longer heard the squeaking and hissing, and although she was unable to look, it seemed to her that the mice had been frightened by the noise of the shattering glass and crept back into their holes.

But what now? Right behind Marie strange sounds were heard in the cabinet, and delicate little voices whispering:

> *"Awake awake.*
> *On to the fight, this very night.*
> *Awake awake."*

At the same time there was a delightful sound of bells. "Oh, that's my little music box," cried Marie happily, and she jumped to one side. Then she saw a strange glow inside the toy cabinet. The whole population seemed to be on the move. A number of dolls were running in all directions, thrashing about with their little arms. All at once, Nutcracker

sat up, threw off his blanket, and jumped out of bed with both feet at once, shouting at the top of his lungs:

"*Crack crack crack,*
Ugly stupid mice,
We'll beat them blue and black,
We'll squash them all like lice,
Crack crack crack."

With that, he drew his little sword, swung it through the air, and cried, "My dear vassals, friends and brothers, will you stand by me in this bitter battle?"

Instantly, three scaramouches, a pantaloon, four chimney sweeps, two zither players, and a drummer shouted, "Yes, Your Lordship—we will follow you through thick and thin, to death, victory, and battle"— whereupon, imitating the intrepid Nutcracker, they jumped from the upper shelf.

It was easy enough for them to jump, as they were fully dressed in

silk and wool, and besides there was nothing much inside them but cotton and sawdust, so they just plumped down like sacks of wool. But poor Nutcracker would certainly have broken his arms and legs, because—just imagine—it was nearly two feet from the shelf where he had been standing to the lowest one, and his body was as brittle as if it had been made of linden wood. Yes, Nutcracker would undoubtedly have broken his arms and legs if, just as he leaped, Mistress Clara hadn't jumped up from the sofa and caught the hero, drawn sword and all, in her arms.

"Ah, my dear sweet Clara," cried Marie through her tears. "How unkind I was to you. I'm sure you were perfectly willing to give friend Nutcracker your bed." But Mistress Clara, pressing the young hero to her silken bosom, said:

"Oh, my lord, I beseech you, sick and wounded as you are, go not into the perilous battle. See how your brave vassals are mustering their forces, eager for the fray and confident of victory. Scaramouche, Pantaloon, Chimney Sweep, Zither Player, and Drummer are already below, and the banner bearers here on my shelf are already on the move. I entreat you, my

lord, to rest in my arms, or to look down upon your victory from the brim of my plumed hat."

So spoke Clara, but Nutcracker was so restive and flailed about so with his legs that Mistress Clara had to put him down on the floor. He knelt graciously and whispered, "My lady, the favor you have shown me will be ever present in my mind on the battlefield."

Clara bent low, took hold of his arms, lifted him gently, quickly undid her spangled girdle, and tried to put it around his shoulders. But he took two steps back, laid his hand on his breast, and said solemnly:

"Dear lady, do not waste this mark of favor upon me, for..." He stopped, gave a deep sigh, quickly tore from his shoulders the ribbon Marie had tied around him, pressed it to his lips, put it on as a token, and, bravely brandishing his bare sword, jumped as nimbly as a bird over the ledge of the cabinet to the floor.

You have surely observed, dear reader, that Nutcracker, even before coming fully to life, had been well aware of Marie's love and regard for him. Of course, it was only because he had become so fond of Marie that he hadn't wanted to accept Mistress Clara's ribbon, shiny and pretty as it was. Faithful Nutcracker preferred to wear Marie's simpler little ribbon.

But what's going to happen now? The moment Nutcracker jumped, the squeaking and squealing started in again. Under the big table, the murderous hordes of mice came to a halt, and over them all towered the hideous mouse with the seven heads. What will happen now?

The Battle

TRUSTY VASSAL-DRUMMER," cried Nutcracker in a loud voice, "sound the advance!" Whereupon the drummer began to ply his drumsticks so skillfully that the windows of the toy cabinet rattled and resounded. A crackling and clattering were heard from inside, and Marie saw the lids of all the boxes where Fritz's army was quartered for the night burst open. Soldiers climbed out and jumped to the bottom shelf, where they formed ranks. Nutcracker ran back and forth, shouting words of encouragement to the troops.

"Why doesn't that dog of a trumpeter bestir himself?" he cried angrily. Then turning to Pantaloon, whose long chin was wobbling badly and who had turned deathly pale, Nutcracker said gravely: "General, I know how brave and experienced you are. What's needed here is a quick eye and the ability to take prompt action. I put you in command of our cavalry and artillery. You won't need a horse. You gallop very nicely on those long legs of yours. Ply your trade."

Pantaloon put his long bony fingers in his mouth and blared as piercingly as a hundred trumpets. A neighing and stamping were heard in the cabinet; Fritz's dragoons and cuirassiers, and most particularly his shiny new hussars, came marching out and halted on the floor down below. With banners flying and bands playing, regiment after regiment marched past Nutcracker and massed in the middle of the room. Fritz's artillery came clanking past. A few moments later the guns were going boom boom. Marie saw sugar balls landing in the serried ranks of the mice, who were spattered with white powder, which made them feel very sheepish. But the worst damage was done by a battery of heavy guns set up on Mama's footstool, which fired jawbreakers—poom poom poom in quick succession—at the mice, many of whom were laid low. But the mice advanced irresistibly and overran some of the artillery positions. Such was the confusion, and such were the smoke and dust, that Marie could hardly see what was going on. But this much was certain: both sides fought with grim determination, and for a long while victory hung in the balance. The mice brought up more and more troops, and the little silver pills that they hurled powerfully and accurately with their sling-shots penetrated even to the glass-fronted cabinet.

Clara and Trude ran about in despair, wringing their hands till they were sore.

"Shall I, the most beautiful of dolls," cried Clara, "die in the bloom of my youth?"

"Was it to perish within these four walls," sighed Trude, "that I have preserved my youthful bloom down through the years?" Then they fell on each other's necks and cried so loud that they could be heard above the din of battle. For, dear listener, you can have no idea of the hubbub that now broke loose. Biff boom clatter bang went the guns and muskets, and through it all the King of the Mice and his henchmice squeaked and screamed. Nutcracker's mighty voice could be heard shouting useful orders, while he himself could be seen striding amid his battalions in the thick of the fire.

Pantaloon had led several brilliant cavalry charges and covered himself with glory, but Fritz's hussars were bombarded by the mouse artillery with nasty, foul-smelling pellets that made horrid spots on their little red jackets. After that they lost all desire to advance. "Column left, march!" cried Pantaloon. In the enthusiasm of giving orders, he too wheeled about to the left, and so did his cuirassiers and dragoons; in other words, they all column-left-marched and went home.

This exposed the battery on the footstool, and it wasn't long before a large body of very ugly mice attacked so ferociously that the whole footstool, guns, gunners, and all, toppled over.

In consternation Nutcracker ordered his right wing to fall back. An experienced soldier like you, Fritz, knows that falling back is pretty much the same as running away, and I'm sure you feel as bad as I do about the misfortunes of Marie's beloved Nutcracker and his army.

But avert your eyes from this sorry situation and turn to the left wing of Nutcracker's army, where things are still going well and there is still ground for hope. In the heat of battle, masses of mouse cavalry had been quietly emerging from under the chest of drawers and had flung themselves with bloodcurdling squeaks on the left wing of Nutcracker's army.

But what resistance they encountered! Slowly, because of the difficult terrain—the ledge of the glass-fronted cabinet had to be negotiated—the banner regiment, led by two Chinese emperors, had advanced and formed a square. These intrepid and magnificently uniformed troops, consisting of gardeners, Tyroleans, Tunguses, barbers, harlequins, cupids, lions, tigers, and monkeys, fought with coolness, courage, and perseverance. With their Spartan bravery, this elite regiment would have wrested the victory from the enemy, had not a daring mouse captain leaped into the fray and bitten the head off one of the Chinese emperors, who in falling crushed two Tunguses and a monkey. This created a gap, through which the enemy advanced, and soon the whole banner regiment was bitten to pieces. But the enemy gained little by their fiendish cruelty, for every time a mouse cavalryman murderously bit one of his valiant adversaries through the middle, a printed label stuck in his throat and he died on the spot.

But this was little help to Nutcracker's army, which, having once begun to fall back, retreated farther and farther, with greater and greater losses, until the unfortunate Nutcracker found himself hard against the toy cabinet with a handful of followers.

"Bring up the reserves!" he cried. "Pantaloon, Scaramouche, Drummer, where are you?" He was still hoping for fresh troops from the cabinet.

And true enough, a few brown men with gold faces, hats, and helmets came out, but they wielded their swords so clumsily that, far from hitting any of the enemy, they knocked off General Nutcracker's cap. It wasn't long before the enemy chasseurs had bitten their legs off, and in toppling over they killed a number of Nutcracker's men.

Hemmed in on all sides, Nutcracker was in dire peril. He tried to jump over the ledge of the toy cabinet, but his legs were too short. Clara and Trude were lying in a faint and could not help him. Hussars and dragoons leaped nimbly past him into the cabinet. In wild despair he shouted: "A horse, a horse! My kingdom for a horse!"

At that moment two enemy musketeers seized him by his wooden cloak and, squeaking triumphantly from his seven throats, the King of the Mice charged him. Marie was beside herself. "Oh, my poor Nutcracker! My poor Nutcracker!" she sobbed. Without quite knowing what she was doing, she took off her left shoe and flung it with all her might into the thick of the enemy, hoping to hit their king. At that moment, everything vanished from Marie's sight. She felt a sharp pain in her left arm and fell to the floor in a faint.

Marie's Illness

W HEN MARIE AWOKE from her deep, deathlike sleep, she was lying in her little bed. The sun was shining into the room, sparkling on the ice-coated windowpanes. A strange gentleman was sitting beside her, but she soon recognized him as Dr. Wendelstern. "She's awake," he said softly. Her mother came over and gave her an anxious, questioning look. "Oh, Mother dear," Marie whispered. "Have all the nasty mice gone away? Was Nutcracker saved?"

"Don't talk such nonsense, child," said her mother. "What have mice got to do with Nutcracker? Oh, you naughty child, we've been so worried about you. That's what happens when children are headstrong and disobey their parents. Last night you stayed up till all hours playing with your dolls. You were sleepy, and a mouse may have come out and frightened you, though I can't believe we have any of those in the house. Be that as it may, you stuck your arm through the glass of the toy cabinet and cut it so badly that Dr. Wendelstern, who has just taken several pieces of glass out of the wound, says that if an artery had been cut you'd have been left with a stiff arm for life or might even have bled to death. Thank heaven I woke up at midnight and wondered where you were. I went into the living room and found you lying beside the cabinet in a faint, bleeding terribly. I was so frightened that I almost fainted myself. There you lay, and all around you I saw Fritz's soldiers and a lot of dolls, broken banners, and gingerbread men. Nutcracker was lying on your bleeding arm, and your left shoe was on the floor nearby..."

"Oh, Mother, Mother," Marie broke in. "There had just been a big battle between the dolls and the mice. The reason I was so scared was that the mice were going to capture poor Nutcracker, who was in command of the dolls. So I threw my shoe at the mice, and after that I don't know what happened."

Dr. Wendelstern gave Marie's mother a meaning look, and she said softly to Marie, "Never mind now, dear child. Don't worry, the mice are all gone, and Nutcracker is safe in the toy cabinet."

Then Marie's father came in and had a long talk with Dr. Wendelstern. He felt Marie's pulse, and she heard some talk of "wound fever."

SHE HAD TO STAY in bed and take medicine, and that went on for several days, though apart from some slight pain in her arm she didn't feel sick or uncomfortable. She knew that Nutcracker had come out of the battle safely, and sometimes she seemed, as if in a dream, to hear him saying to her quite distinctly: "Marie, dearest lady, I am deeply indebted to you, but you can do even more for me." She wondered what that might be, but in vain. She couldn't think of anything.

She couldn't play properly because of her sore arm, and when she tried to read or leaf through her picture books, everything looked so hazy that she had to stop. Time hung heavy on her hands, and she could hardly wait till nightfall, because then her mother sat down beside her bed and told her beautiful stories. She had just told her the excellent story of Prince Fakardin when the door opened and Godfather Drosselmeier stepped in, saying, "It's high time that I saw for myself how my poor little Marie is getting along."

The moment Marie saw Godfather Drosselmeier in his short yellow

coat, she seemed to see Nutcracker fighting his losing battle with the mice, and without thinking she cried out, "Oh, Godfather Drosselmeier, how ugly you were! I saw you sitting on the clock, covering it with your wings to keep it from striking aloud, because that would have scared the mice away—I heard you calling the King of the Mice. Oh, why didn't you come to Nutcracker's help, you nasty Godfather Drosselmeier. It's all your fault that I hurt myself and have to lie here sick in bed."

Marie's mother was horrified. "Dear child," she said, "what are you talking about?" But Godfather Drosselmeier made strange faces and said in a rasping, monotonous voice:

> "Pendulum had to whir, softly purr
> And couldn't strike
> That's how pendulums are.
> But bells are ringing
> Ding dong, bing bong, bing bong.
> Doll girl, don't be frightened,
> Bells are ringing loud and long
> To chase the King of Mice away
> Owl comes flying black and gray
> Pick peck, pick and peck,
> Bells are ringing, clocks are whirring
> Pendulums can't help whirring
> Snick and snack, whir and purr."

Marie stared wide-eyed at Godfather Drosselmeier, because he looked entirely different and much uglier than usual and was moving his right arm back and forth like a marionette. She would have been really afraid of him if her mother hadn't been there and if Fritz, who had turned up in the meantime, hadn't interrupted him with loud laughter and cried out:

"Goodness gracious, Godfather Drosselmeier, you're really funny today. You make me think of the jumping jack that I threw behind the stove the other day."

But the children's mother said very gravely, "Dear Judge Drosselmeier, what a strange rigmarole! What is the meaning of it all?"

"My word," said Drosselmeier, laughing. "Didn't you know my pretty watchmaker's song? I always sing it to little patients like Marie."

With that he sat down at Marie's bedside and said, "Don't be cross with me for not putting out all fourteen of the Mouse King's eyes. That wasn't possible. Instead, I've brought you something that will really give you pleasure."

With that, he reached into his pocket, and guess what he took out—Nutcracker, whose lost teeth he had put back in very neatly and firmly, and whose broken jaw he had fixed as good as new. Marie cried out for joy, but her mother said with a smile:

"You see how good Godfather Drosselmeier is to your Nutcracker."

"And, Marie," the Judge broke in, "you'll have to admit that Nutcracker is no great beauty. Now, if you like, I shall tell you how such ugliness came into his family. Oh yes, it's been handed down from generation to generation. Or maybe you already know the story of Princess Pirlipat, the witch Mouserinks, and the clever clockmaker?"

"Hey, Godfather Drosselmeier," Fritz interrupted, "you've put Nutcracker's teeth in just right, and his jaw isn't as wobbly as it was, but why hasn't he got a sword? Why haven't you given him one?"

"My dear boy," said Drosselmeier testily, "you always have to complain. Why should I worry about Nutcracker's sword? I've cured his bodily ills; it's up to him to find himself a sword if he wants to."

"That's a fact," said Fritz. "If he's worth his salt, he'll get himself the weapons he needs."

"All right, Marie," the Judge went on. "Tell me if you know the story of Princess Pirlipat."

"No, I don't. Oh, tell it, Godfather Drosselmeier."

"I hope," said the child's mother, "I do hope, dear Judge, that this story won't be as gruesome as your stories usually are."

"Oh no, dear lady," said Drosselmeier. "On the contrary, this is a fairy story."

"Oh, tell it, tell it, dear Godfather," the children cried. And the Judge began.

The Story of the Hard Nut

PIRLIPAT'S MOTHER was a king's wife. That made her a queen, and the moment she was born Pirlipat was a princess. The king was beside himself with joy over his beautiful daughter, who lay in her cradle. He cheered and danced and hopped about on one foot, and shouted over and over again:

"Hurrah! Has anyone ever seen anything as beautiful as my little Pirlipat?"

And all his ministers, generals, counselors, and staff officers hopped about on one foot like their sovereign, and shouted: "No! Never!"

And indeed it was undeniable that no more beautiful child than Princess Pirlipat had been born since the world began. Her little face might have been woven of the finest lily-white and rose-red silk, her eyes were like sparkling azure stones, and her curly locks were like threads of gold. What's more, little Pirlipat was born with two rows of pearly white teeth, with which, two hours later, she bit the Lord Chancellor's finger when he bent low to get a closer look at her features, making him scream "Oh, jiminy!", though it is also claimed that he just said, "Ouch!" On this score opinions are divided to this day, but Pirlipat definitely bit the chancellor's finger, and the whole kingdom was delighted at this indication that spirit, energy, and perspicacity were housed in Pirlipat's exquisite little frame.

In short, everyone was happy. Only the queen seemed troubled, though no one knew why. For one thing, she arranged for Pirlipat to be closely guarded. In addition to the sentries at the doors and two ladies-in-waiting sitting close to the baby's cradle, there had to be six nurses in the room at night. But what seemed utterly absurd and beyond understanding was that each of the six nurses had to hold a tomcat on her lap and stroke him so busily all night that he would never stop purring. Dear children, you couldn't possibly guess why Pirlipat's mother had to take all these precautions, but I know, and I'll tell you without delay.

On a certain occasion a number of excellent kings and charming princes had foregathered at the court of Pirlipat's father. Brilliant entertainment was provided, including tournaments, comedies, and balls. To show that he had adequate supplies of gold and silver, the king had decided to dig deeply into the royal treasury and treat his guests to something really splendid. So, when the royal head cook informed him that the court astronomer had informed *him* that the time was right for pork butchering, the king resolved to provide a sumptuous sausage feast. He hopped into his carriage and drove about, personally inviting all the kings and princes to "a simple spoonful of soup," as he put it—for he wished to enjoy their surprise. And then he said amiably to the queen, "You know, my dear, how I like sausages prepared."

The queen knew exactly what he meant. He meant that she herself should perform the useful duty of sausage making, as she had done on other occasions. The Chancellor of the Exchequer was ordered to remove the big golden sausage kettle and the silver casseroles from the great treasury vault and send them to the kitchen. A great fire was made of sandalwood. The queen put on her damask apron, and soon the kettle was steaming with delicious sausage broth, whose fragrance penetrated even to the council chamber. Overcome with delight, the king could not control himself. "Just a moment, gentlemen!" he cried, and he ran to the kitchen, hugged the queen, and stirred the kettle for a moment with his golden scepter. That calmed him, and he went back to the council chamber.

The critical moment came when the fat had to be cut into small cubes and browned on silver spits. The ladies-in-waiting withdrew, because the queen, out of love and respect for her royal husband, wished to perform this task alone. But when the fat began to sizzle, a faint whisper was heard. "Sister," said the voice, "give me some of that. I'm a queen too, and I too want something good to eat."

The queen knew who it was. It was Madam Mouserinks, who had been living in the royal palace for many years and claimed to be related to the royal family. She called herself the queen of Mousolia and had a large retinue under the stove. The queen was a kindly woman. Though unwilling to acknowledge Madam Mouserinks as her sister, she was glad to let her share in the feast. "Very well, Madam Mouserinks," she said. "Come right out. Of course you may have some of my crispy fat."

So Madam Mouserinks came hopping out, jumped up on the stove, and with her pretty little paws grabbed one little cube of fat after another as the queen forked them out to her. But then all Madam Mouserinks's aunts and uncles came running, and even her seven sons, who were dreadful little rascals. They flung themselves on the fat, and the terrified queen found it impossible to fend them off. Luckily, the head lady-in-waiting came in and chased the intruders away before the fat was all gone. The court mathematician was called in, and what was left of it was carefully divided in accordance with his calculations.

DRUMS ROLLED and trumpets blared. The princes and potentates appeared in their resplendent robes of state, some on white palfreys, others in crystal coaches. Crown on head and scepter in hand, the king welcomed them and took his seat at the head of the table. During the liver-sausage

course the king became visibly pale and his eyes turned heavenward. Sighs escaped from his breast; some unspeakable pain seemed to be gnawing at his vitals. But during the blood-sausage course he sobbed and groaned and slumped in his chair, burying his face in his hands.

Everyone jumped up. The court physician tried in vain to feel the unfortunate king's pulse. Some deep, mysterious suffering seemed to be tearing him to pieces. Drastic remedies—feather quills and the like— were attempted. The queen pleaded with him to tell her what was wrong. At length he seemed to recover a little, and muttered almost inaudibly: "Not enough fat."

In despair the queen fell at his feet, sobbing. "Oh, my poor unfortunate royal husband!" she cried. "Oh, what sufferings you have endured. You see the culprit here at your feet. Punish her, punish her severely. Alack alas! Madam Mouserinks with her seven sons and her aunts and uncles ate up the fat and..." With that, the queen fell back in a faint.

The king jumped up in a rage and cried aloud, "Chief lady-in-waiting, how did this happen?"

The chief lady-in-waiting told him as much as she knew, and the king resolved to avenge himself on Madam Mouserinks and her family, who had eaten the fat that should have been in the sausage. The privy council was summoned, and it was decided that Madam Mouserinks should be tried for her life and that all her property should be confiscated. But since the king feared that she might go on eating his fat in the meantime, the whole matter was referred to the court clockmaker and wizard.

This man, whose name was the same as mine, Christian Elias Drosselmeier, promised to drive Madam Mouserinks and her family from the palace forever by an act of astute statesmanship. What he actually did was invent certain ingenious machines, to which small pieces of fat were attached by threads, and place them all over Madam Mouserinks's apartment. Madam Mouserinks was far too shrewd to be enticed by Drosselmeier's contraptions, but all her warnings, all her remonstrances, were in vain. Lured by the pungent smell of browned fat, all seven sons and any number of aunts and uncles went straight to Drosselmeier's engines of destruction. When they tried to nibble the fat, a gate suddenly fell and they were captured, whereupon they were taken to the royal kitchens and ignominiously executed.

Gathering what was left of her family, Madam Mouserinks left the scene of her cruel loss. Her heart was filled with rage, despair, and thirst for vengeance. The court rejoiced, but the queen lived in fear, for she knew Madam Mouserinks like a book and felt sure she wouldn't take the death of her sons and relations lying down. True enough, Madam Mouserinks appeared in the kitchen just as the queen was cooking kidney stew for her husband, who was especially fond of that dish, and said, "My sons, aunts, and uncles have been slain. Take care, Your Highness, that the queen of the mice doesn't bite your little princess in two. Take care!"

With that she vanished and was seen no more, but the queen was so frightened that she dropped the kidney stew in the fire. That was the second time Madam Mouserinks had ruined one of the king's favorite dishes, and it made him very angry.

"Well, that's enough for tonight. I'll tell you the rest another time."

Much as Marie, who had ideas of her own about this story, begged Godfather Drosselmeier to go on, he sprang to his feet, saying, "Too much at a time wouldn't be good for you. I'll tell you the rest tomorrow."

As the Judge was leaving the room, Fritz asked him, "Tell me, Godfather Drosselmeier, is it really true that you invented mousetraps?"

"How can you ask such a silly question?" said Mrs. Stahlbaum. But the Judge smiled strangely and said, "Do you think an ingenious clockmaker like me would be incapable of inventing a mere mousetrap?"

The Story of the Hard Nut, Continued

N OW, CHILDREN," Judge Drosselmeier continued the next evening: Now you know why the queen had the beautiful Princess Pirlipat guarded so closely. Can you blame her for being afraid that Madam Mouserinks would carry out her threat and bite the little princess to death? Drosselmeier's machines were of no use at all against the wily Madam Mouserinks. But the court astronomer, who was at the same time the privy astrologer, argued that Purr and Tomcat and his family had the power to keep Madam Mouserinks away from the cradle. Accordingly, each of the nurses had to hold a scion of that family—the whole lot of them were employed at court as legation secretaries—on her lap, and sweeten his arduous duty by diligently scratching his back.

Once night at exactly twelve o'clock, a lady-in-waiting who was sitting close by the cradle was startled from a deep sleep. All was quiet round about. Not a purr could be heard. In that deathly stillness you might have heard the woodworm nibbling in the wainscoting. Imagine how this lady-in-waiting must have felt when she saw a big ugly mouse standing up on its hind legs with its hideous head right on top of the princess's face. The lady jumped up with a cry of horror, waking every-

body else, but at that moment Madam Mouserinks (for the big mouse beside Pirlipat's cradle was none other) scurried into the corner. The legation secretaries ran after her, but too late; she had vanished into a crack in the floor. Awakened by the noise, little Pirlipat cried pitifully.

"Thank goodness she's alive!" cried the nurses. But what was their horror when they looked at Pirlipat and saw what had become of the lovely, delicate child. Instead of the angelic red-and-white face framed in golden curls, they saw an ungainly fat head on a tiny shrunken little body; the azure-blue eyes had been changed into staring green popeyes, and the sweet little mouth had become a gash stretching from ear to ear.

The queen almost died of grief, and the walls of the king's study had to be covered with cotton batting because he kept ramming his head against them, wailing in the most pitiful voice, "Oh, what an unhappy monarch I am!"

He might have realized by then that it would have been better to eat his sausages without fat and to leave Madam Mouserinks and her tribe in peace under the stove. But that wasn't how Pirlipat's royal father's mind worked. He simply put all the blame on the royal clockmaker and wizard, Christian Elias Drosselmeier of Nuremberg, and issued a decree giving Drosselmeier four weeks to restore Princess Pirlipat to her former state or at least suggest a surefire means of doing so, failing which, he should suffer a shameful death at the hands of the royal executioner.

Drosselmeier was terrified. But then, trusting in his craft and in his luck, he did what seemed to be the first thing to do. He skillfully took Princess Pirlipat apart, unscrewed her hands and feet, and examined her inner structure. Unfortunately, he discovered that the larger she grew the more hideous she would be, and he could think of no remedy for it. So he carefully put the princess together again, and, sitting beside her cradle, which he was not allowed to leave, he sank into deepest gloom.

THE FOURTH WEEK had already begun. Indeed, it was already Wednesday of that week when the king, his eyes flashing with rage, looked in, shook his scepter with all his might, and cried out, "Christian Elias Drosselmeier, cure the princess or you must die."

Drosselmeier wept bitter tears, but Princess Pirlipat just cracked nuts. For the first time the wizard was struck by Pirlipat's unusual appetite for nuts, and also noticed that she had come into the world with teeth. The fact of the matter was that immediately after her transformation she had begun to cry, and she had cried until a nut happened to come her way. In a trice she had cracked the nut and eaten the kernel. That calmed her, and from then on her nurses had thought it wise to keep her supplied with nuts.

"O holy natural instinct, O eternally inscrutable sympathy of all

49

beings," cried Christian Elias Drosselmeier. "Thou hast shown me the door to the secret; I shall knock at that door and it will open."

He asked leave to take counsel of the court astronomer, and was brought to him under heavy guard. The two wise men embraced and wept, wept and embraced, for they were dear friends. Then they withdrew to a secret chamber and consulted numerous books dealing with instinct, sympathies, antipathies, and other mysterious things. Night fell. The astronomer gazed at the stars and, with the help of Drosselmeier, who was also versed in such matters, drew up Princess Pirlipat's horoscope. This was no easy matter, for the lines of her destiny crisscrossed and tangled, but at last—oh joy!—at last it was clearly revealed that all Princess Pirlipat had to do to throw off the spell that had made her ugly and to recover her beauty was to eat the sweet kernel of the nut Krakatuk.

The nut Krakatuk had so hard a shell that a field howitzer could ride over it without cracking it. This hard nut had to be cracked in the princess's presence by the teeth of a man who had never shaved and never worn boots, and this young man would have to hand her the kernel with his eyes closed and not open them until he had taken seven steps backward without stumbling.

DROSSELMEIER and the court astronomer had been hard at work for three whole days and nights. That Saturday the king had just sat down to his noonday meal when Drosselmeier, who was scheduled to be beheaded on Sunday, burst joyously into the room and announced that he had discovered the way to restore Princess Pirlipat's lost beauty. The king embraced him rapturously and promised him a diamond sword, four medals, and two new Sunday coats.

"I expect you," he added affably, "to get to work right after lunch. Just see to it, my dear wizard, that an unshaven young man in shoes is on hand with the nut Krakatuk. And don't give him any wine to drink beforehand,

50

because we don't want him stumbling when he takes seven steps backward like a crab; afterwards he can get as drunk as he likes."

The king's words filled Drosselmeier with consternation. Trembling and quaking, he explained to the king that though the means had been revealed, both the nut Krakatuk and the young man who could crack it with his teeth remained to be looked for, and it was doubtful whether nut and nutcracker would ever be found.

The king, in a towering rage, swung his scepter over his crowned head and roared with the voice of a lion:

"In that case we'll go through with the beheading!"

Luckily for the terrified Drosselmeier, the king had enjoyed his lunch most especially that day and was therefore disposed to heed the sensible advice that the magnanimous queen, who was touched by Drosselmeier's plight, did not fail to give him. Drosselmeier took heart and argued that he had indeed discovered the means by which the princess could be saved and therefore deserved to have his life spared. "Stuff and nonsense!" said the king. But after downing a glass of schnaps he decided that the two of them, the clockmaker and the astronomer, should set out and not come back till they had the nut Krakatuk. The man who was to crack the nut would—as the queen suggested—be found through advertisements in the local and foreign newspapers.

HERE THE JUDGE broke off again and promised to finish the story the following evening.

The Story of the Hard Nut, Concluded

THE CANDLES had just been lit the next evening when Godfather Drosselmeier did indeed arrive in Marie's room and resume his story:

DROSSELMEIER and the court astronomer had been traveling from place to place for fifteen years, and still they had discovered no trace of the Nut Krakatuk. Children, I could spend four weeks telling you about all the places they went and all the strange and unusual things that happened to them, but I won't. Instead, I shall tell you only that Drosselmeier was sick at heart and longed for his beloved native city of Nuremberg. One day when he and his friend were smoking wretched tobacco in the middle of a large forest in Central Asia, Drosselmeier was quite overpowered by homesickness. "O Nuremberg," he cried—

> "O Nuremberg my happy home
> How foolish I have been to roam
> And how I yearn to return
> To Nuremberg, my Nuremberg
> Where houses all have windows
> And churches all have doors."

As Drosselmeier kept lamenting and lamenting, the astronomer, overcome with sympathy, began to moan so pitifully that he could be heard all over Asia. But after a while he pulled himself together, wiped his tears, and said, "Dear and esteemed colleague, why do we sit here lamenting? Why don't we go to Nuremberg? What difference does it make where we look for that wretched nut Krakatuk?"

"You've got something there," replied Drosselmeier, and heaved a sigh of relief. They both arose, knocked the ashes out of their pipes, and headed straight for Nuremberg. They had barely arrived when Drosselmeier ran to his cousin, the carver, varnisher, and gilder of dolls, Christoph Zacharias Drosselmeier, whom he had not seen for many years. The clockmaker told the doll maker the whole story of Princess Pirlipat, Madam Mouserinks, and the nut Krakatuk. The doll maker clapped his hands in amazement and cried out, "Cousin, cousin, how perfectly wonderful!"

The clockmaker also related the incidents of his long journey, how he had spent two years with the King of Dates, how the Prince of Almonds had rudely turned him away, how he had vainly consulted the Natural History Society in Squirrelville—in short, how he had nowhere found the slightest trace of the nut Krakatuk.

While listening, Christoph Zacharias had several times snapped his fingers, twirled about on one foot, and clicked his tongue. In the end he exclaimed, "Hmm!—Good gracious!—Heavens above!—I can hardly believe it!" Then he tossed his cap and wig into the air, hugged his cousin with all his might, and cried out, "Cousin! Cousin! You're a made man! Because if I'm not very much mistaken, the nut Krakatuk is right here in my house."

Whereupon he brought in a box, opened it, and took out a gilded, medium-sized nut.

"Here it is," he said. "And now let me tell you how I came by it. Many years ago, at Christmastime, a strange man came here with a sack full of nuts that he was trying to sell. Right outside my shop he got into a fight with a local nut seller, who felt very strongly that a stranger had no business selling nuts in our town. So the stranger put down his sack, and just then a heavily loaded cart came along and rode over it. All his nuts were cracked except one, which the vendor offered with a mysterious smile to sell me for a 1720 twenty-kreuzer piece. I looked in my pocket and to my great surprise found just the coin the man wanted. So I bought the nut and gilded it. I can't imagine why I paid so much for that nut and why I prized it so highly."

Every last doubt about its being the precious nut Krakatuk was dispelled when the court astronomer scraped away the gilt and found the word "Krakatuk" incised in the shell in Chinese characters. The travelers were overjoyed, and the doll maker was the happiest of men when his cousin Drosselmeier assured him that his fortune, too, was assured, since, in addition to a sizable pension, he would be supplied with gold for his gilding as long as he lived.

The two travelers, the wizard and the astronomer, had already put on their nightcaps and were getting ready for bed when the astronomer spoke up as follows:

"Esteemed colleague, one piece of good fortune never comes alone. Take my word for it, the nut Krakatuk isn't the only thing we've found; we've also found the young man who's going to crack it between his teeth and give Princess Pirlipat the beauty kernel. I am referring to none other than your cousin's son." And in his enthusiasm he protested: "No, I will not go to bed. I mean to draw up the young man's horoscope this very night."

With that he threw off his nightcap and set to work on his observations.

True enough, the cousin's son was an affable, nice-looking young

fellow who had never been shaved and had never worn boots. In his younger days, to be sure, he had been a jumping jack for a Christmas or two, but all trace of that had vanished, for since then his father had taught him proper behavior. Now, at Christmastime, he wore a sword and a red jacket with gold trimmings; and since he carried his hat under his arm, there was nothing to hide his magnificent pig-tailed wig. There he stood in his father's shop, gallantly cracking nuts for young ladies, for which reason they called him Nutcracker.

Next morning, the astronomer threw his arms around the clockmaker and cried out, "It's him! We've got him, he's found. But there are two things, my dear colleague, that must be borne in mind. First, you must make your excellent nephew a sturdy wooden pigtail, connected with his lower jaw in such a way that a tug at the one sets the other in motion; second, when we return to the palace, we must take care not to tell a soul that we have brought the young man who is to crack the nut with his teeth; in fact, he must not show himself until we have been there for some time. I read in the horoscope that after a few others have broken their teeth trying to crack the nut, the king will promise the princess and his throne to the man who succeeds and thereby restores the princess's lost beauty."

Cousin doll maker was so delighted to hear that his son was going to marry Princess Pirlipat and become a prince and a king that he entrusted the boy entirely to the care of the two travelers. The pigtail that Drosselmeier attached to his hopeful young nephew was a complete success, and thanks to this device the boy was able to crack the hardest peach pits.

Drosselmeier and the astronomer sent word to the palace that the nut Krakatuk had been found, and advertisements were put in the papers forthwith. By the time the travelers got there, several handsome young men, including one or two princes, had arrived, determined, thanks to the soundness of their teeth, to free the princess from the witch's spell. The travelers were aghast when they saw the princess. The little body with its tiny hands and feet could barely support the ungainly head. The ugliness of the face was accentuated by a white cotton beard that had sprouted over her mouth and chin.

Everything happened as the astronomer had read in his horoscope. One beardless and bootless boy after another broke his teeth and jaws on the nut Krakatuk without doing the princess the least bit of good. When carried away semiconscious by the dentists who were in attendance for the occasion, they sighed, "That is indeed a hard nut to crack!"

The king in despair then promised his daughter and kingdom to the man who would break the spell, whereupon the gentle and well-bred young Drosselmeier stepped forward and asked leave to try. None of the young men had made such an impression on the princess. She pressed her little hands to her heart and sighed ever so fervently: "Oh, I do hope it's he who cracks the nut and becomes my husband."

After young Drosselmeier had graciously saluted the king and queen and Princess Pirlipat as well, the Lord High Chamberlain handed him the nut Krakatuk. He put it between his teeth, gave his pigtail a good tug, and—crack crack—broke the shell into many pieces. Adroitly removing a few fibers from the kernel, he handed it to the princess with a low bow, closed his eyes, and took a step backward. The princess swallowed the kernel, and wonder of wonders! The misshapen monster was no more, and there stood the loveliest of maidens. Her face was woven of lily-white and rose-red silk; her eyes were glittering azure stones; and her head was piled high with curled threads of gold.

Drums and trumpets mingled with the rejoicings of the populace. The king and his whole court danced on one foot, as they had at Pirlipat's birth, and the queen, who had fainted for joy, had to be rubbed with cologne. The tumult was most upsetting to young Drosselmeier, who had still to complete his seven steps backward. But he kept his head, and was just raising his right foot for the seventh step when Madam Mouserinks arose from the floor, piping and squeaking hideously. In putting his foot down, young Drosselmeier stepped on her, and almost fell.

Oh, cursed fate! A fraction of a moment later, young Drosselmeier was as ugly as Princess Pirlipat had been. His shrunken body could hardly support the monstrously swollen head with the big protuberant eyes and the wide, hideously yawning mouth. In place of his pigtail he now had a narrow wooden cloak with which to move his lower jaw. Both the clockmaker and the astronomer were beside themselves with horror, but then they saw Madam Mouserinks on the floor, writhing in her blood. Her wickedness had not gone unavenged, for young Drosselmeier's toe had struck her so sharply in the neck that she was doomed to die. But in her death agony Madam Mouserinks squeaked in a most heartrending manner:

> *"O Krakatuk, hard nut from which I die*
> *Hee hee, pee pee*
> *You too, Nutcracker, will perish by and by.*
> *My son with sevenfold crown*
> *Will bring Nutcracker down.*
> *Yea, never fear*
> *He will avenge his mother dear.*
> *O Life, blood red and milky white,*
> *I leave thee for the shades of night.*
> *Squeak!"*

With that last cry Madam Mouserinks expired. She was carried away by the Keeper of the Royal Stoves. No one had been paying attention to young Drosselmeier, but then the princess reminded the king of his promise, and he gave orders to bring the young hero in. But when the poor fellow appeared thus disfigured, the princess held her hands before her

face and cried out: "Take him away. Take that nasty Nutcracker away!"

Without delay the Royal Bouncer seized him by his little shoulders and threw him out the door. The king was furious at this attempt to palm a nutcracker off on him as a son-in-law. He put all the blame on the clockmaker and the astronomer, and banished them both from his kingdom forever. This last development was not in the horoscope that the astronomer had drawn up in Nuremberg. But that did not discourage him from making further observations, and he read in the stars that young Drosselmeier would make the best of his new situation and become a prince and a king despite his ugliness. But, the horoscope continued, he would cast off his ugliness only if he could kill the son whom Madam Mouserinks had borne after the death of her seven sons with their seven heads, and if he could win a lady's heart in spite of his ugliness. And it seems that young Drosselmeier, as most recently seen in his father's shop in Nuremberg, is a nutcracker but also a prince.

That, children, is the story of the hard nut, and now you know why people say, that was a hard nut to crack, and why it is that nutcrackers are so ugly.

THE JUDGE had finished his story. In her opinion, said Marie, Princess Pirlipat was a horrid, ungrateful minx. Fritz, however, thought that if Nutcracker had an ounce of spunk he would make short shrift of the King of the Mice and get his good looks back.

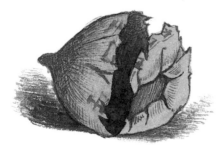

Uncle and Nephew

IF ANY OF MY esteemed readers or listeners has ever chanced to cut himself on glass, he will know how painful it is and how wretchedly long such cuts take to heal. Marie had to stay in bed for almost a week, because she was dizzy whenever she got up. But after a while she felt better and was able to run around the house as merrily as ever. The toy cabinet looked lovely with its fresh new trees and houses and dolls. And what pleased her most of all was seeing her beloved Nutcracker, who stood on the second shelf and displayed an excellent mouthful of teeth when he smiled at her. But then, as she was feasting her eyes on him, she suddenly realized to her consternation that Godfather Drosselmeier's whole story had been the story of Nutcracker and his battle with Madam Mouserinks and her son.

Now she knew that her Nutcracker could be none other than young Drosselmeier from Nuremberg, Godfather Drosselmeier's charming nephew, who, unfortunately, had been transformed by Madam Mouserinks's magic. For even while listening to the story, Marie hadn't doubted for one moment that the skillful clockmaker at the court of Pirlipat's father was none other than the Judge himself.

"But why didn't your uncle help you? Why didn't he help you?" she lamented, as it became clearer and clearer to her that the battle she had witnessed had been a battle for Nutcracker's crown and kingdom. Hadn't all the other dolls been his subjects? And wasn't it as sure as anything could be that the court astronomer's horoscope had come true and that young Drosselmeier had become King of the Dolls?

As clever Marie pondered all this, thinking of Nutcracker and his subjects as living and breathing, it seemed to her that they ought really to live and breathe. But they did nothing of the kind. The inhabitants of the toy cabinet remained lifeless and still, but now, far from going back on what she staunchly believed, she blamed their lifeless condition on the magic spells of Madam Mouserinks and her seven-headed son.

"But never mind," she said aloud to Nutcracker. "Even if you can't move or say the least little word to me, Mr. Drosselmeier, I know you see into my heart and know how devoted I am to you. Count on my help if you need it—at the very least, I'll ask your uncle to help you with his skill when necessary."

Nutcracker didn't budge, but it seemed to Marie that the gentlest of sighs came to her almost inaudibly, but ever so sweetly, through the glass panes, and that a little bell-like voice sang to her:

"*Dear, sweet Marie,*
Protectress mine.
Thou standest by me
And I'll be thine."

Marie took a strange pleasure in the cold shivers that ran down her spine.

By then it was dusk. Dr. Stahlbaum came in with Godfather Drosselmeier, Louise set the tea table, and soon the family was sitting around it, talking of pleasant things. Marie quietly pulled up her little easy chair and sat at Godfather Drosselmeier's feet. In a moment when none of the

61

others was saying anything, she looked straight into the Judge's face with her big blue eyes and said:

"Dear Godfather Drosselmeier, now I know that my Nutcracker is your nephew, young Drosselmeier from Nuremberg. He became a prince, or rather a king—it all came out just as your friend the astronomer predicted. But you certainly know that he's at war with Madam Mouserinks's son, the ugly King of the Mice. So why don't you help him?"

Marie went on to tell the whole story of the battle as it had looked to her, and was often interrupted by the laughter of her mother and Louise. Only Fritz and Drosselmeier remained unsmiling.

"Where on earth does the child get such crazy ideas?" asked the doctor.

"Oh," said Mrs. Stahlbaum, "she has always had a lively imagination. Actually, I think it's dreams brought on by her fever."

"I don't believe it," said Fritz. "My red hussars can't be such cowards. They'd hear from me if they behaved like that."

But Godfather Drosselmeier, smiling strangely, picked Marie up on his lap and spoke to her more gently than ever before:

"Ah, my dear little Marie, you're luckier than I or anyone else. You're a born princess like Pirlipat, for you rule over a fresh and beautiful country. But you will have much to suffer if you mean to befriend the poor misshapen Nutcracker, for the King of the Mice will beset him wherever he goes. But there's nothing I can do—you alone can save him. So be steadfast and loyal."

Neither Marie nor any of the others knew what Drosselmeier meant by these words. Indeed, Dr. Stahlbaum thought them so strange that he felt the Judge's pulse and said, "Dear friend, you are suffering from cerebral congestion. I'll write you out a prescription."

But the doctor's wife shook her head thoughtfully and said, "I have an idea what the Judge is getting at, but I can't quite put it into words."

Victory

I T WASN'T LONG before Marie was awakened in the moonlight by a strange rumbling that seemed to come from one corner of her room. It was as though pebbles were being thrown and rolled about, and at the same time she heard the nastiest whistling and squeaking.

"Oh dear, the mice are here again!" Marie cried out in a fright. She tried to call her mother, but she couldn't make a sound or stir a muscle. And then she saw the King of the Mice squeeze through a hole in the wall. With flashing eyes and crowns he scurried across the floor and jumped up on the little table beside Marie's bed. "Hee hee hee," piped the King of the Mice, "give me your sugar balls, give me your marzipan, or I'll bite your Nutcracker to pieces." And then, gnashing his teeth most abominably, he slipped into a hole in the wall.

Marie was so frightened by the gruesome apparition that she was very pale the next morning and could hardly say a word. A hundred times she was about to tell her mother or Louise or at least Fritz what had happened, but then she thought: "Will anyone believe me? Won't they just laugh at me?"

Still, it was plain to her that to save Nutcracker she would have to sacrifice her sugar balls and marzipan. So that night she put her whole supply of these delicacies at the foot of the toy cabinet.

Next morning her mother said: "I can't understand how all those mice could get into our living room. Look, my poor Marie, they've eaten up all your sweets."

And so they had. The gluttonous King of the Mice hadn't found the marzipan to his liking but had gnawed at the edges with his sharp teeth, so it had to be thrown away. Marie didn't mind about the candy; actually, she was delighted, for she thought she had saved Nutcracker. So imagine how she felt that night when she heard the squeaking and squealing close to her ears. The King of the Mice was back again. His eyes flashed even more dangerously than the night before, and he whistled even more disgustingly between his teeth: "Give me your sugar dolls, or I'll bite your Nutcracker to pieces." And with that the horrid King of the Mice scurried away.

Marie was miserable. Next morning she went to her cupboard and looked sadly at her sugar dolls. And she had good reason to be sad, for you can't imagine, attentive reader, what sweet little figures, all carved and molded from sugar, little Marie Stahlbaum owned. There was a handsome shepherd with his shepherdess, tending a flock of milk-white sheep, while his dear little dog capered around them; there were two postmen striding along with letters in their hands; and there were four of the prettiest couples, sprucely dressed young gentlemen and daintily dressed young ladies, swinging in a Russian swing. There were some dancers, and behind them William Tell and the Maid of Orléans, who didn't mean much to Marie, but in the far corner stood a red-cheeked child, Marie's favorite. The tears came to Marie's eyes. "Oh!" she cried, turning to Nutcracker. "Dear Mr. Drosselmeier, I'll do anything I can to save you, but it's very hard."

Nutcracker looked so pathetic that Marie, who seemed to see the

Mouse King's seven mouths open wide, ready to gobble the poor boy up, decided to sacrifice every one of her sugar dolls. So that night she set them all in front of the toy cabinet, as she had her sweets the night before. She kissed the shepherd, the shepherdess, and the lambs, and last of all the red-cheeked child. But she put the child in the last row. William Tell and the Maid of Orléans were up front.

"This is dreadful," cried Mrs. Stahlbaum the next morning. "There must be some horrid big mouse living in the toy cabinet, because all of poor Marie's sugar dolls have been nibbled and bitten."

Marie couldn't hold back her tears, but she soon smiled again, for she thought: "What does it matter, since Nutcracker is saved?"

That evening when Mrs. Stahlbaum was telling the Judge about the mischief a mouse had done in the children's toy cabinet, the doctor blurted out, "It's really too bad we can't get rid of that wretched mouse that's eating up all Marie's candy."

"I've got it," Fritz broke in. "The baker downstairs has an excellent gray legation secretary. I'll bring him up here, and he'll soon bite the mouse's head off, even if it's Madam Mouserinks herself or her son the King of the Mice."

"Won't that be lovely!" said Mrs. Stahlbaum, laughing. "And he'll prowl around on the chairs and tables and knock all the cups and glasses over and do all sorts of damage."

"Not at all," said Fritz. "The baker's legation secretary is as clever as they make them. I wish I could walk on the crest of the roof the way he does."

"Please, no cats in the house at night," begged Louise, who couldn't abide cats.

"Actually," said the doctor, "Fritz is right. But we could set a trap instead. Haven't we got one?"

"Godfather Drosselmeier will make us one," cried Fritz. "He invented them." All laughed. And when Mrs. Stahlbaum informed them that there was none in the house, the Judge said he had several, and within the hour he had an excellent mousetrap brought from his own home.

Fritz and Marie had their heads full of the Judge's story about the hard nut. When Dora the cook was browning the fat, Marie trembled, and, her mind filled with the story and its marvels, she said to Dora, whom she had known for years: "Oh, Your Majesty. Beware of Madam Mouserinks and her family." Fritz drew his sword and cried, "Let them come! I'll give them more than they bargained for." But all remained quiet under the stove and on top of it.

As the Judge was fastening the fat to a thin wire and ever so quietly putting the trap down next to the toy cabinet, Fritz cried out:

"Take care, Godfather Clockmaker, that the Mouse King doesn't play some trick on you."

OH, WHAT A TIME Marie had that night! Something ice-cold scurried about on her arm, something rough and disgusting lay down on her cheek and piped and squeaked in her ear. The horrid King of the Mice sat down on her shoulder; blood-red foam poured from all seven of his mouths, and, gnashing and grinding his teeth, he piped and squeaked in her ear:

"Hiss hiss hiss
Stay away from that house
Mustn't get caught,
O precious mouse
You'll have to miss
The feast.
Give us your picture books
Give us your little dresses
Or you'll have no peace.

Nutcracker will be eaten alive.
Hee hee pee pee
Squeak!"

Marie was beside herself with anguish. And the next morning she was pale and distraught when her mother said, "That nasty mouse hasn't been caught." But believing that Marie was upset about her sweets and afraid of the mouse, her mother added, "Don't worry, child. We'll get rid of that wicked mouse. If the traps don't help, Fritz can bring in his gray legation secretary."

No sooner was Marie alone in the parlor than she went to the toy cabinet and, sobbing, said to Nutcracker, "Oh, dear Mr. Drosselmeier, what can I do for you, poor unhappy child that I am? If I give that horrid Mouse King all my picture books and even the beautiful dress the Christ Child brought me, he'll just keep asking for more. I won't have anything left, and instead of you he'll want to bite me to pieces. Oh, poor me, what shall I do?"

While thus weeping and lamenting, Marie noticed a big bloodstain on Nutcracker's neck. It had been there since the eventful night. Now that she knew that her Nutcracker was really young Drosselmeier, the Judge's nephew, she no longer carried him about in her arms and had given up kissing and fondling him. Indeed, she felt rather shy about touching him altogether. Today, however, she took him carefully out of the cabinet and began to rub off the bloodstain with her handkerchief. Imagine how she felt when she suddenly noticed that Nutcracker was growing warmer in her hand and starting to move. Quickly she put him back on his shelf. And then his lips stirred and he said in a strained whisper:

"Oh, dear Mistress Stahlbaum, honored friend, I already owe you so much. You mustn't sacrifice your picture books or your little Christmas dresses on my account. Just get me a sword; a sword is all I need, I can manage the rest even if he . . ."

At that his words ebbed away, and his eyes, which had been alive with the most fervid melancholy, became fixed and dead. Marie felt no fear. On the contrary, she danced for joy, for now she knew a way of saving Nutcracker without any more painful sacrifices. But where was she to find the little fellow a sword?

She decided to ask Fritz for advice, and that evening when their parents had gone out and the two children were sitting by themselves beside the glass cabinet in the living room, she told him the whole story of Nutcracker and the King of the Mice and explained what was needed to save Nutcracker.

What upset Fritz the most was hearing from Marie's lips that his hussars had given such a poor account of themselves in the battle. He asked her in dead earnest if that was really true, and when she gave him her word that it was, he went straight to the cabinet and treated his hussars to a stirring harangue. To punish them for their cowardice, he cut the insignia off their caps one by one and forbade their band to play the "Hussars' March" for exactly one year. After thus discharging his disciplinary duties, he finally turned to Marie.

"I can get Nutcracker a sword," he said, "because only yesterday I pensioned off an old colonel of the cuirassiers. He won't be needing his fine sharp sword anymore."

The colonel in question was living on his pension in the hindmost corner of the third shelf. Fritz took him out, relieved him of his silver saber, and slung it around Nutcracker's waist.

THE NEXT NIGHT fear and dread kept Marie awake. At the stroke of twelve, she seemed to hear strange sounds, a clanging and a crashing, in the parlor. And then suddenly: "Squeak!"

"The Mouse King! The Mouse King!" cried Marie. Stricken with horror, she jumped out of bed.

All was still. But soon she heard a soft knocking at the door and a faint little voice:

"Esteemed Mistress Stahlbaum, open the door and have no fear. I bring good news!"

Recognizing young Drosselmeier's voice, Marie threw on her dressing gown and opened the door. There stood Nutcracker, holding the bloody sword in his right hand and a wax candle in his left. The moment he saw Marie, he went down on his knee and said:

"You alone, dear lady, gave me the courage and strength to fight the insolent varlet who dared to defy you. The treacherous King of the Mice has been vanquished and lies writhing in his blood. Deign, dear lady, to accept these tokens of victory from the hand of one who will be your true and faithful knight until death."

With that, Nutcracker adroitly stripped off the Mouse King's seven golden crowns, which he had been wearing on his left arm, and handed them to Marie, who accepted them with delight. Then Nutcracker rose to his feet and continued:

"Oh, Mistress Stahlbaum, what splendid things I can show you in this hour of victory over my enemy, if you will be kind enough to follow me a little way. Come with me, I beg you, dear Mistress."

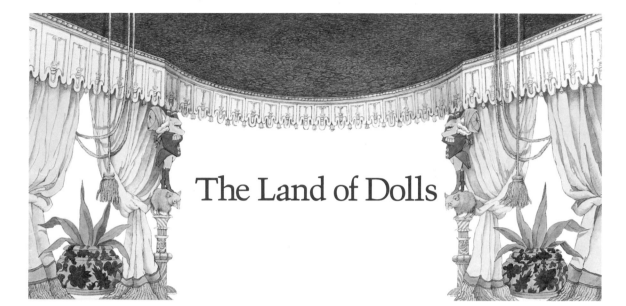

The Land of Dolls

I DON'T THINK any of you children would have hesitated for a moment to follow the honest, good-natured Nutcracker, who never had a wicked thought in all his life. And Marie was all the more inclined to go with him as she knew what a debt of gratitude he owed her and was sure that he would keep his word and show her all manner of splendid things. So she said:

"I'll go with you, Mr. Drosselmeier, but don't let it be too far or take too long, because I haven't had enough sleep yet."

"In that case," Nutcracker replied, "I'll take the shortest route, though it's rather a hard one."

He went ahead and Marie followed. He finally stopped outside the big clothes cupboard in the entrance hall. To Marie's surprise, the door of the cupboard was wide open, and she could see her father's fox-fur traveling coat, which was hanging at the front of the cupboard. Nutcracker climbed nimbly, hanging on to the loops and trimmings, until he was able to get hold of the big tassel that was fastened by a heavy cord to the back of the coat. When he pulled the tassel, a little cedarwood ladder came down through the sleeve.

"Now, Mistress Stahlbaum," said Nutcracker, "if you'd just climb that ladder..."

Marie climbed and soon passed through the sleeve. When she looked out through the neckhole, a bright light met her eyes and she found herself in a fragrant meadow, dotted with millions of gemlike sparks.

"This is Candy Meadow," said Nutcracker. "But in a moment we'll pass through that arch."

Looking up, Marie saw the beautiful arch, which was only a few steps away. It appeared to be made of white, brown, and raisin-colored marble, but when she went closer she saw that it was actually made of baked almonds and raisins, for which reason, as Nutcracker informed her, it was called Almond and Raisin Arch. The arch was enriched by a gallery that seemed to be made of sugar, and on it six little monkeys in red jackets were playing Turkish music. The music was so beautiful that Marie hardly noticed the pavement they were walking on, which looked like mottled marble, but was really made of artfully molded nougat. Soon she was surrounded by sweet smells given off by the woods on either side of the path. Glittering lights in the dark foliage proved to be gold and silver fruits hanging from stems of many different colors. The trunks and branches were decorated with ribbons and bunches of flowers like the members of some joyful wedding party. When the orange-scented zephyrs stirred, the leaves and branches rustled, and the tinsel tinkled and crackled like merry music, to which the sparkling lights hopped and danced. Marie was in seventh heaven.

"Oh, it's so wonderful here," she sighed.

"This, Mistress," said Nutcracker, "is Christmas Wood."

"Oh," said Marie, "if I could only stay here awhile. Oh, it's so lovely."

Nutcracker clapped his hands, and several little shepherds and shepherdesses, hunters and huntresses appeared, all so white you'd have thought they were made of pure sugar. They had all been strolling about

in the woods, but Marie hadn't noticed them before. Now they brought up a dear little golden chair, put in a white licorice cushion, and ever so graciously bade Marie be seated. She had no sooner done so than the shepherds and shepherdesses danced a charming ballet, while the hunters played ever so genteelly on their horns. But then, as if at a signal, they all vanished into the woods.

"I beg your pardon," said Nutcracker. "I humbly beg your pardon, dear Mistress Stahlbaum, that the ballet should have ended so wretchedly. But you see, these performers are all members of our mechanical ballet, so they can only do the same thing over and over again. And if the hunters played so sleepily and feebly, there are reasons for that too. It's true that the candy basket hangs right over their noses on Christmas trees, but a little too high, a little too high...But suppose we go on a little way?"

"I thought it was all perfectly lovely," said Marie, getting up and following Nutcracker. They skirted a gently whispering brook, which seemed to be the source of all the delightful smells the woods were full of.

"This is Orange Brook," said Nutcracker. "It smells good, but it's not nearly as big and beautiful as Lemonade River. They both empty into Almond Milk Lake."

And indeed Marie soon heard a louder gurgling and splashing and saw the broad Lemonade River flowing in great biscuit-colored waves between banks covered with bushes that glittered like rubies. It gave off a cooling freshness that strengthened heart and lungs. Not far away a dark yellow stream dragged itself sluggishly along. But the scent it gave off was uncommonly sweet. Beautiful children were sitting on its banks, fishing for plump little fishes, which they ate the moment they caught them. When she came closer, Marie noticed that the fishes looked like hazelnuts.

A little way downstream there was a sweet little village. Houses, church, parsonage, barns, all were dark brown, but roofed with gold. And many of the walls looked as if the mortar had been studded with shelled almonds and candied lemon peel.

"That's Gingerbread City," said Nutcracker. "It's on Honey River. The inhabitants are beautiful, but most are dreadfully cranky because they have awful toothaches, so we won't stop there now."

Just then Marie caught sight of a town made up of varicolored, transparent houses. When they reached it, Marie heard a merry hubbub and saw thousands of lovely little people unloading heavy wagons that were drawn up in the marketplace. What they hauled from the wagons looked like colored paper and chocolate bars.

"This is Candytown," said Nutcracker. "A shipment has just arrived from Paperland and the King of Chocolate. The poor Candytowners have received threatening messages from the Prince of Mosquitoes, so now

they're covering their houses with special paper and building fortifications with the finely wrought tablets sent by the King of Chocolate. But, my dear Mistress Stahlbaum, we can't visit every small town and village in this country. The capital is the place. On to the capital!"

Nutcracker hurried ahead, and Marie, bursting with curiosity, followed. Soon the air was filled with the scent of roses and everything seemed covered with a soft roseate glow, reflected, as Marie could see, from a rose-red stream, whose silvery-rose waters lapped and gurgled most musically. Gradually, the stream widened and became a lake with silvery-white swans floating on it. They wore gold necklaces and vied with one another in singing the prettiest songs, while diamond fish leaped in and out of the rosy waters in a merry dance.

"Oh!" cried Marie in delight. "This is the lake Godfather Drosselmeier was going to make for me, and I'm the little girl who was going to pat the swans."

Nutcracker smiled as though she had said something foolish.

"Uncle could never make a lake," he said. "You yourself would be much more likely to. But instead of worrying our heads over that, let's sail across this rosy lake to the capital."

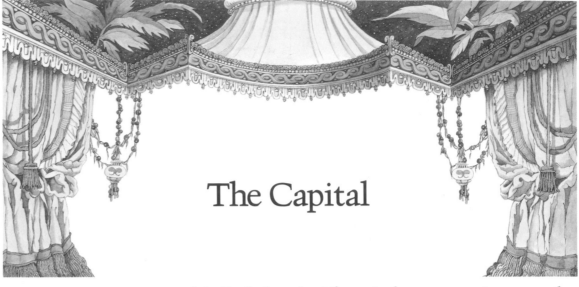

The Capital

NUTCRACKER CLAPPED his little hands. The wind came roaring over the lake and the waves rose higher. A gondola made entirely of glittering jewels appeared in the distance and quickly came closer. It was drawn by two dolphins with golden scales. Twelve dear little Moors with caps and little aprons woven of gleaming hummingbird feathers leaped ashore and carried first Marie, then Nutcracker to the gondola, which quickly started off again.

Oh, how lovely it was for Marie to glide over the waters in the gondola, with the scent of roses all about her and the rosy waves below. The two golden dolphins raised their nostrils and spouted crystal streams high into the air. And as the spray fell in filmy rainbows, two silvery voices sang:

> *"Who is this on the rosy water?*
> *A fairy or a fairy's daughter?*
> *Bim-bim little fishes,*
> *Sim-sim golden swans.*
> *Fairies come hither,*
> *Fly through the spray*

Splish splash, splish splash
The rosy spray."

But the twelve little Moors, who had jumped up on the back of the gondola, seemed to take offense at the singing streams of water, for they shook their parasols so violently that the palm leaves they were made of rattled. And at the same time, they stamped their feet in a strange rhythm and sang:

> "Klip klop, klip klop
> Down and up.
> Blackamoors' feet must never stop,
> Swans and fishes, wiggle and glide,
> Gondola must smoothly ride.
> Klip klop, klip klop."

"Those Moors are all very well," he said, "but if they keep that up they're going to make the whole lake rebellious."

And true enough, a deafening hubbub broke out—a medley of strange voices that seemed to be partly in the air and partly in the water. But Marie paid no attention to them, for she was looking into the fragrant rosy waves, from each of which a charming little girl's face smiled at her.

"Oh!" she cried, clapping her little hands. "Look, Mr. Drosselmeier, Princess Pirlipat is down there. She's smiling at me as sweetly as can be. Oh, dear Mr. Drosselmeier, do look and see."

But Nutcracker sighed almost sorrowfully and said, "Dear Mistress Stahlbaum, that's not Princess Pirlipat, that's you, your own self; it's your own sweet face smiling at you out of the waves."

At that Marie raised her head, closed her eyes tight, and felt ashamed. And just then the twelve little Moors lifted her out of the carriage and carried her ashore.

She found herself in a small thicket that was almost more beautiful than the Christmas Wood. Everything in it sparkled and glittered. But most wonderful of all were the strange, wondrously colored fruits, which gave off a delicious fragrance.

"This," said Nutcracker, "is Marmalade Grove, and over there you see the capital."

And what did Marie see? How shall I even begin to describe the beauty and splendor of the city that now lay before her on a broad flowery plain. Not only were the walls and towers of the most magnificent colors, but the shapes of the buildings were like nothing else on earth. For instead of roofs the houses wore delicately plaited crowns, and the towers were wreathed in varicolored foliage. As the two of them emerged from the city gateway, which looked as if it had been made of macaroons and candied fruits, silver soldiers presented arms and a little man in a brocade dressing gown threw his arms around Nutcracker and said:

"Welcome, noble Prince, welcome to Candytown."

Marie was not a little surprised that so very distinguished a person should recognize Drosselmeier as a prince. But then she heard so many fine little voices clamoring all at once, such rejoicing and laughter, such singing and playing, that she forgot everything else, and she had to ask Nutcracker what it all meant.

"Oh, most-honored Mistress Stahlbaum," Nutcracker replied, "there's nothing unusual about it. Candytown is a big bustling city, it's like this every day. Let's just go on a little farther."

They had taken only a few steps when they came to a large market-place that was most amazing to behold. The houses around it were all made of sugar filigree. There were whole tiers of arcades, and in the middle stood an obelisk of cake with white icing, around which four beautifully carved fountains spouted orangeade, lemonade, and other tasty sweet drinks, and the basin was full of custard that you might have eaten with a spoon. But prettiest of all were the delightful little people, thousands of whom came thronging together from all sides, laughing and singing and joking—in short, the merry hubbub that Marie had heard in the distance. There were beautifully dressed ladies and gentlemen, there were Armenians and Greeks, Jews and Tyroleans, officers and common soldiers, clergymen, preachers and shepherds and clowns, as many different kinds of people as there are in the world.

On one corner the tumult was wilder than elsewhere. People were scattering in a panic, because the Grand Mogul was being carried past in a litter, escorted by ninety-three grandees of the empire and seven hundred slaves. But it so happened that on the next corner five hundred members of the Fishermen's Guild were putting on their annual parade,

and unfortunately the Sultan of Turkey had taken it into his head to come riding across the marketplace at that very moment with three thousand Janissaries. To make matters worse, the grand procession of the "Interrupted Sacrifice" came along at the same time. The band played and the adepts marched toward the obelisk, intoning their hymn: "Arise, give thanks to the Sun."

The result was a pushing and shoving and squeaking. Soon there were cries of lamentation, for in the crush a fisherman had knocked a Brahman's head off and the Grand Mogul was almost run down by a clown. People were beginning to punch and pound one another when the man in the brocade dressing gown, who had hailed Nutcracker as a prince, climbed up on the obelisk. An extraordinarily loud bell was rung three times, and he cried aloud: "Pastrycook! Pastrycook! Pastrycook!"

Instantly, the hubbub died down; the processions disentangled themselves as best they could, the soiled Mogul was brushed off, and the Brahman's head was pasted back on. Whereupon the same merry hubbub as before began all over again.

"Dear Mr. Drosselmeier," Marie asked, "what's all this about a pastrycook?"

"Ah, Mistress Stahlbaum," Nutcracker replied. "Here the name of Pastrycook is given to an unknown but cruel spirit, which is thought to have total power over people. It is the destiny that governs this merry little nation, and the people stand so much in awe of it that, as the Lord Mayor has just shown, the wildest disorders can be quelled by the mere mention of the name. When that happens, no one thinks of earthly matters such as pokes in the ribs or clouts over the head; everyone looks within and says to himself: What is man? And what can be done with him?"

Marie could not repress a cry of surprise and admiration when she saw before her a castle with a hundred lofty towers bathed in a roseate glow. Now and then splendid bouquets of violets, daffodils, tulips, and gillyflowers were strewn over its walls, accentuating the pinkish whiteness of the background with their glowing dark colors. The gigantic dome of the central building and the pyramidal roofs of the towers were sprinkled with thousands of gold and silver stars.

"This," said Nutcracker, "is Marzipan Castle." Marie lost herself in contemplation of the magic castle, but it didn't escape her that one of the main towers had no roof and that some little men, perched on a scaffolding of cinnamon sticks, were evidently trying to put one on. But before she had time to question Nutcracker, he explained:

"Not so long ago this castle was threatened with destruction. The giant Sweettooth came along, gobbled up the roof of that tower, and was nibbling at the big dome. The citizens of Candytown bought him off by offering him a whole precinct of the city and a considerable part of

Marmalade Grove. The giant accepted the offer, gorged himself, and went on his way."

At that moment soft music was heard, the gates of the castle opened, and out stepped twelve pages holding lighted clove sticks as torches. Their heads were pearls, their bodies rubies and emeralds, and they tripped along on beautifully worked little feet of pure gold. After them came four ladies almost as big as Marie's Clara, but so richly and splendidly attired that Marie knew they could only be princesses. After embracing Nutcracker tenderly, they cried out:

"O my Prince! My beloved Prince! O my brother!"

Nutcracker seemed deeply moved. He wiped floods of tears from his eyes, took hold of Marie's hand, and said with great feeling:

"This is Mistress Marie Stahlbaum, the daughter of an eminent physician. She saved my life. If she hadn't thrown her slipper at the right time, if she hadn't outfitted me with the pensioned colonel's sword, I'd be

lying in my grave, bitten to pieces by the abominable King of the Mice. Tell me now, can Pirlipat, though a true princess, hold a candle to Mistress Stahlbaum for beauty, kindness, and virtue? No, I say, she cannot!"

All the ladies exclaimed: "No!" and fell on Marie's neck, gasping through their sobs:

"O noble savior of our beloved princely brother! Excellent Mistress Stahlbaum!"

The ladies led Marie and Nutcracker to an inner room, whose walls were made of sparkling colored crystal. But what Marie liked best about the place were the dear little chairs, tables, bureaus, writing desks, and so on, all made of cedar or Brazil wood strewn with golden flowers. The princesses bade Marie and Nutcracker be seated and announced their intention of preparing a meal with their own hands. First they set out lots of little dishes and bowls of the finest Japanese porcelain, and plenty of spoons, knives, forks, graters, casseroles, and other kitchenware, all of gold and silver. Then they brought in the most wonderful fruit and candy Marie had ever seen and began with their little snow-white hands to squeeze the fruit, crush the spices, and grate the sugared almonds. In short, they did all they could to show Marie what first-rate cooks they were and what a splendid meal she could look forward to. Knowing that she, too, was well versed in such matters, she secretly wished that she could be allowed to give the princesses a hand.

As though reading Marie's mind, the most beautiful of Nutcracker's sisters handed her a little golden mortar, saying: "Dear sweet friend, you who saved our brother's life, would you care to pound some of this rock candy?"

While Marie pounded the rock candy, so cheerfully that the mortar murmured a kind of song, Nutcracker related slowly and at great length the history of the cruel war between the Mouse King's army and his own—how the cowardice of his troops had brought about his defeat, how the hideous King of the Mice had been on the point of biting him to pieces and Marie had been obliged to sacrifice a good many of his subjects who were in her service, etc.

As Marie listened to his story, it seemed to her that his words and even the strokes of her pestle sounded more and more faint and distant. Soon she saw silvery mists, which seemed to rise up and engulf the princesses, the pages, Nutcracker, and herself. She heard a strange singing and whirring and buzzing, which ebbed away in the distance. Higher and higher she rose, as though on mounting waves—higher and higher and higher.

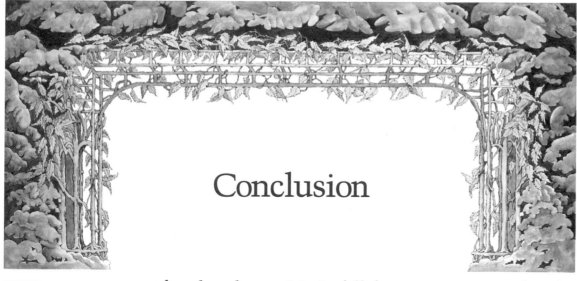

Conclusion

THEN CAME a poof and a plop as Marie fell from an immense height. My, what a tumble!

When she opened her eyes, she was lying in her little bed. It was broad daylight, and her mother was standing there.

"How can anyone sleep so long!" her mother exclaimed. "Breakfast was ready long ago."

Of course, dear reader, you realize that Marie, befuddled by all the wonderful things she had seen, had finally fallen asleep in Marzipan Castle and that the pages, or possibly even the princesses themselves, had carried her home and put her to bed.

"Oh Mother, dear Mother, you can't imagine all the places young Mr. Drosselmeier took me to last night and all the beautiful things I've seen."

Then she told the whole story almost exactly as I've just told you. Her mother looked at her in amazement.

"You've had a long, beautiful dream, dear Marie, but now you must really forget all that nonsense."

When Marie went on insisting that it wasn't a dream, that she had really seen all those things, her mother took her to the glass-fronted cabinet, pointed at Nutcracker, who was standing on the third shelf as usual, and said, "Silly child, how can you imagine that this wooden doll from Nuremberg is really alive and capable of moving about?"

"But, Mother dear," said Marie, "I *know* Nutcracker is young Mr. Drosselmeier from Nuremberg, Godfather Drosselmeier's nephew."

Dr. and Mrs. Stahlbaum burst out laughing. Marie was on the verge of tears. "Oh, Father dear, now you're even laughing at my Nutcracker, and he spoke so well of you. When we came to Marzipan Castle and he introduced me to the princesses his sisters, he referred to you as an eminent physician."

The laughter grew louder. Louise and even Fritz joined in. Marie ran to the other room, brought back her little box, took out the Mouse King's seven crowns, and handed them to her mother.

"Look, Mother. These are the Mouse King's seven crowns, which young Mr. Drosselmeier gave me last night in token of his victory."

Mrs. Stahlbaum looked in amazement at the seven crowns, which were made of some sparkling metal, worked more skillfully than seemed possible for human hands. When the doctor, too, had feasted his eyes on the little crowns, both father and mother urged Marie to tell them where they had come from. But the child could only repeat what she had said before, and when her father scolded her severely and went so far as to call her a liar, she burst into tears and cried out, "Oh dear! Oh dear! What do you want me to say?"

At that moment the door opened. The Judge came in, saying, "Oh oh! What's going on? What has made my beloved godchild cry?"

The doctor told him the whole story and showed him the little crowns. The Judge took one look at them and said:

"Stuff and nonsense! Stuff and nonsense! These are the little crowns I used to wear on my watch chain. I gave them to Marie for her second birthday. Don't you remember?"

Neither Dr. nor Mrs. Stahlbaum remembered a thing. But when

Marie saw her parents smiling again, she took courage, ran up to Godfather Drosselmeier, and said:

"You know everything, Godfather Drosselmeier. Won't you please tell them that my Nutcracker is your nephew, young Mr. Drosselmeier from Nuremberg, and that he gave me the little crowns?"

But the Judge made a stern face and muttered, "Stuff and nonsense!" And Dr. Stahlbaum looked severely at his daughter and said, "Look here, Marie. You're to forget about this foolishness once and for all. And if I ever again hear you saying this ugly, simpleminded Nutcracker is Judge Drosselmeier's nephew, I'll throw Nutcracker out of the window and all your other dolls as well, including Mistress Clara."

After that, of course, Marie couldn't say another word about her adventures, though her heart was still full of them, for as you can easily imagine, it's not so easy to forget such grand and beautiful things as Marie had seen. Even—esteemed reader or listener Fritz—even your friend Fritz Stahlbaum turned his back on his sister Marie whenever she began to tell him about the wonderful country where she had been so happy. He is even said to have muttered once or twice between his teeth, "Silly goose!" In view of his usual good nature, I find this hard to believe. But this much is certain—from then on he ceased to believe anything Marie told him. He formally apologized to his hussars for the injustice he had done them, replaced the insignia he had taken away from them with tall goose plumes, and gave them leave to play the "Hussars of the Guard" march again. Which was all well and good, but you and I know what a sorry figure the hussars cut when the nasty pellets began making spots on their red tunics.

THOUGH FORBIDDEN to speak of her adventure, Marie continued to be haunted by memories of the fairyland she had seen. Whenever she turned her mind to it, she saw it all again, and instead of playing as usual, she would sit still for hours, deep in thought. The others all scolded her and called her a little dreamer.

One day the Judge happened to be repairing one of the Stahlbaum clocks. Marie was sitting by the glass-fronted cabinet, lost in her dreams and gazing at Nutcracker. Suddenly, quite of their own accord, the words popped out of her:

"Oh, dear Mr. Drosselmeier, if you were really alive, I wouldn't be like Princess Pirlipat. I wouldn't scorn you because you had stopped being a handsome young man on my account."

On hearing that, the Judge exploded: "Stuff and nonsense!" But in that same moment, there was such a bang and jolt that Marie fell in a faint from her chair. When she came to, her mother was watching her and said, "How can a big girl like you fall off her chair like that?—The Judge's nephew from Nuremberg is here. So be on your good behavior."

Marie looked up. The Judge had put his glass wig and his yellow coat back on and was smiling happily. He was holding by the hand a small but shapely young man with a little face as white as milk and as red as blood. He was wearing a magnificent red coat trimmed with gold, and white silk stockings and slippers, and amidst the ruffle of his shirt he was carrying a charming bouquet. He was elegantly curled and powdered and had a splendid pigtail hanging down behind. The little sword at his side sparkled as if it were made all of jewels, and the little hat under his arm was woven of silk fibers. The young man had charming manners, which he displayed by bringing Marie all sorts of lovely toys, figures of the finest marzipan, including those that the King of the Mice had bitten to pieces, and a beautiful saber for Fritz. At the table he obligingly cracked nuts for the whole company; even the hardest could not resist him. With his right hand he put them in his mouth, with his left he pulled his pigtail, and— crack!—the shell broke into pieces.

Marie turned as red as a beet when she saw the young man, and she turned even redder after dinner when young Drosselmeier asked her to go with him to the glass cabinet in the parlor.

"Go and play, children," said the Judge. "Now that my clocks are telling the right time, I have no objection."

NO SOONER was young Drosselmeier alone with Marie than he went down on one knee and said, "Oh, my precious Mistress Stahlbaum, you see at your feet the happiest of men, whose life you saved on this very spot. You were kind enough to say that you would not scorn me as that nasty Princess Pirlipat did, for becoming ugly on your account. In that instant, I ceased to be a lowly nutcracker and regained my former, not unpleasant aspect. Oh, precious Mistress Stahlbaum, favor me with your hand, share my crown and kingdom with me, reign with me over Marzipan Castle, for I am king there now."

Marie raised the young man to his feet and said softly, "Dear Mr. Drosselmeier, you are a good kind gentleman, and since in addition you rule over a charming country full of pretty and amusing people, I accept you as my betrothed."

So then Marie was engaged to Drosselmeier. In a year and a day he called for her in a golden carriage drawn by silver horses. At the wedding, two and twenty thousand of the most brilliant figures adorned with pearls and diamonds danced, and Marie is believed to be still the queen of a country where sparkling Christmas woods, transparent marzipan castles, in short, the most wonderful things, can be seen if you have the right sort of eyes for it.

AND THAT'S the story of Nutcracker and the King of the Mice.

Acknowledgments

ON OPENING NIGHT of the Pacific Northwest Ballet production of *Nutcracker* in Seattle, Washington, I was witness to a tradition that was both beautiful and appropriate. Kent Stowell, artistic director of PNB, led the cast and those artists most directly connected with *Nutcracker* to the footlights and then proceeded to usher out a long line of backstage people without whom this mammoth work would never have been produced. It was a generous, fair gesture, and a delightful one to behold, black ties mingling with blue jeans and paint smocks.

On the stage of the Seattle Opera House stood artists who represented the vast complexity of a production that involved an entire city and a rare combination of the finest technical and graphic artists from America, Canada, and England. Their great number prevents my acknowledging their invaluable help with anything more than a heartfelt salute.

In honor of the fine tradition exemplified that night, I thank the City of Seattle for its communal enthusiasm and financial and moral support.

In keeping with the spirit of this production, I wish also to thank some of those whose artistry and craftsmanship brought *Nutcracker* to life.

Seattle: Jerome Sanford, Shef and Patty Phelps, Jane Lang, Dr. and Mrs. Herschell Boyd, Paula Prewett, Stewart Kershaw, Lisa McCallister, Jeff Lincoln, Peter Gantt, Skip Templeton, Thomas Fichter, Laurel Cancilla, Larae Hascall, Eleanor von Dassow, Wayne Gerou, Rebecca Wakefield, Lisa Havens, Keith Brumley, Mark Zappone, Joan Purswell, Irv Huck, Jane Hayes Andrew, E. J. Schlesinger, Phyllis Herford, Elizabeth Rummage, Lisa Wood, Kristin Fortier, Carol Mockridge, Marlene Moore, Laura Mc-Creery, Jody Allen, Michael McDonald, Howard Neslen, Christopher, Ethan (François), Darren (Jacques), Jan Johnston, Greg Jones, Bob Breeden, Kevin Beaty, Leslie Martin, and the staff and the children of the PNB; *Montreal:* Miles McCarthy, Karen Ryan; *Portland, Oregon:* Scott MacGregor; *New York City:* Ken Billington, Jeffrey Schissler, Grace Costumes, Bruce Harris, Ken Sansone, Rusty Porter, Ed Otto, Sheldon Fogelman; *San Francisco:* Pierre Cayard; *Lewes, Sussex, England:* Paul Fowler.

My very special gratitude goes to: Peter Horne, Michael Hagen, Sandra Woodall, Randy Chiarelli, and Murray Johnson.

Finally, to Eugene Glynn, Lynn Caponera, Erda and Io, of Ridgefield, Connecticut, all my love.